# VANISHED IN A HEARTBEAT

## HILIARY AMANDA

Thank you ~
Hiliary

*For my husband who pushed me to pursue my dreams*
*For my children who are my inspiration*
*For my parents who encouraged my writing my entire life*
*For my sister who is my biggest cheerleader*
*For my aunt who loves me like a mom*

*In memory of the worlds most incredible grandparents who loved me*
*unconditionally and without walls, making me a better person for it.*

# PREFACE

In a small town in Indiana, there is a beautiful upscale neighborhood filled with mature trees and gorgeous landscaping. Smiling faces and happiness abound as families gather outside, playing with their children and enjoying their lives. Inside the stately neighborhood, on the biggest lot, at the end of the cul-de-sac, sits the largest of the homes. With a perfectly manicured lawn and the most beautiful hydrangeas, any gardener could dream of. Here you will find the neighborhood dream house. This is the home of the Fergusons. Lucas Ferguson, a prominent local defense attorney, married to Abigail, a stay-at-home mom. They have three children: Madison, fourteen; Kaitlyn, ten; and Brody, eight.

To the outside world, they are the epitome of a perfect family, having it all and wanting for nothing. However, behind closed doors, trouble is brewing, threatening to cause this picture-perfect family to implode.

# CHAPTER 1

"Honey, can you help me finish setting up? Allison and Benjamin will be here any minute," Abigail calls from the kitchen while Lucas sits comfortably in the living room on the couch texting.

"Yeah, sure, I will be there in a minute," he replies, distracted.

A few minutes pass before Abigail peeks her head around the corner at Lucas, shaking her head in annoyance.

"Lucas, please," she begs.

Lucas holds up a finger and answers an incoming call. Abigail stands there quietly, listening to her husband on the phone for a few minutes before she goes on to finish getting everything ready for their dinner party- alone. They are having their best friends over for dinner. Allison, Abigail's lifelong best friend, who also happens to live next door, and Benjamin, her husband, someone that has grown to be a good friend of Lucas's. The foursome enjoys hanging out quite often. Tonight, all of Abigail and Lucas's children are staying at their respective friend's houses; therefore, it will be a much-needed adult-only night.

The doorbell rings, and Abigail walks quickly to answer it, looking over her shoulder as she opens the front door. She catches a glimpse of Lucas as he walks towards his office, deep in conversation on the phone. Abigail welcomes her friends in with a big smile and a hearty hug.

"Hey, girl, what's up?" Allison asks while hugging her friend back happily. Benjamin follows his wife inside, offering Abigail a bottle of wine they had brought with them. The trio walks together toward the living room.

"How is it going, you guys have a good week?" Benjamin asks cheerfully.

"It was good, thanks! I am so glad you both could make it! I have been looking forward to tonight all week!" Abigail exclaims, leading the two toward the kitchen. As they walk past the office, Abigail glares at a distracted Lucas while mouthing the words, "Get off the phone," before continuing to the kitchen with their friends.

"Allison, if you help me carry everything into the dining room, we are ready to eat," Abigail states as she grabs two bowls and motions to the remaining platter on the counter while walking into the other room.

"Great, I am starved." Benjamin laughs while rubbing his belly and following behind.

Lucas walks in as the women set the food onto the table and bear hugs Abigail from behind, kissing her on the top of her head. "Sorry, babe, that was important. I am being hired to represent a new client on a complicated murder case. I have to go see him in the jail in the morning."

Abigail stiffens to his touch but slowly finds herself sinking into his embrace. "Let's just have a good time tonight, okay? No more work until the morning."

Lucas just gives her a smile and moves to the head of the table. "Smells delicious honey."

"Hey, man, good to see ya," Benjamin says, slapping Lucas on the back. "Sounds like you have been busy!"

"Always," Abigail responds with a little bit more attitude in her voice than she meant to convey. Trying to recover and not ruin the evening, she smiles and pulls out her chair. "Okay, guys, everything is out. Let's eat!"

The group sits, eats, and chats cheerfully. It has been about a month since they have all gotten together like this, and they had a lot to catch up on. Lucas can feel the piercing glares from Abigail every time he responds to a text. After an hour, the friends move to the living room with their wine and continue their conversations. Everyone is laughing and joking, except for Lucas, who is preoccupied with his phone.

"Dang, Abigail, go easy on the wine there, my friend," Allison jokes as Abigail pours herself another glass.

"Listen here," she scolds. "First night kid-free in I don't know how long, I am drinking all the wine!"

"Speaking of kids, I saw Madison walking around the neighborhood the other day with a boy. Is that the boyfriend I have been hearing about?" Benjamin asks with a smirk.

"Ugggh, yes, I am so not ready to be dealing with her and boys. The other day, they actually tried to sneak off into her room! I about lost my mind," Abigail responds emphatically.

"Better be getting your gun ready there, daddy," Benjamin says, laughing while looking over to Lucas.

To the annoyance of Abigail, Lucas does not look up or respond to the comment. She looks over at her friends, embarrassed, and takes a long swig of her wine. They all sit in silence for a few minutes. Abigail stares intently at him while he continues to text, oblivious to the awkwardness everyone else is feeling around him. Finally, fed up with being ignored, she attempts to get his attention.

"And then, we decided we were not waiting for the train, so

we sped up as fast as we could and jumped the track, right before the train came flying by," she explains sarcastically.

"Um, hmmmm. That's nice," Lucas murmurs back, his head and fingers buried in his phone, texting fervently.

Abigail downs the last of her wine and slams the glass onto the coffee table, causing Allison to jump. "What a surprise! You aren't even listening to me! You *never* listen to me! All you do is mess around on your stupid phone!" Abigail screams, tossing her hands up.

Lucas looks up from his phone, annoyed with his wife, and jumps to his feet, both seeming to forget the company they have sitting just a few feet away.

"You have no idea the stress that I am under and all of the work that I do for this family. My phone is my work, Abbi. I have over one hundred clients right now. That takes up so much of my time!"

"I understand that your job is stressful, but that doesn't give you a free pass to treat the members of your family like total crap. I am tired of you ignoring the kids! Look at how you treat me! If you have too many clients stop taking on new ones, pass them off to other attorneys in your office. You don't have to handle them all on your own."

"*Treat you?*" Lucas says, taken aback. "You are tired of how I *treat* you? What exactly are you tired of Abigail? The nice house in the suburbs, your car, your ability to get whatever you want whenever you want without worry if we can afford it? Where do you think that ability comes from? My work! And for all that work, what do I get from you? Grief! Give me a break!" Lucas goes back to his phone.

Abigail sits there for a few moments, soaking in her husband's outburst. Allison looks at Benjamin, and they both shrug. "Let's just give them a few minutes to deal with whatever that is," Benjamin whispers as they quietly get up and walk out to the backyard.

Abigail watches as her friends walk away, and it fuels her anger, and she unleashes it on her husband.

"Wow, just freaking wow! Are you serious right now? Well, toot toot to you baby, husband of the year right here! You work and support your family. Where should we put your award? Should I put an announcement in the paper, call the news, throw you a party? I mean, no other husband actually goes out and supports his family. What I am asking you to do is *also engage* with your family! When was the last time you even had a meaningful conversation with me that was *not* about one of your stupid cases? When was the last time you did anything with the kids?" Abigail shouts with her arms flailing everywhere.

"I pay for and support all the extracurriculars and fun things that the kids do! They want for nothing; *you* want for nothing!" he shouts back.

"But they *want* to *spend* time with *you*, Lucas! *Time!* We all *want* your time!"

Lucas rubs the bridge of his nose and begins to pace out of anger and exasperation.

"Abigail, at this stage in my career I do not have any more free time. This new client is a very sensitive and difficult case, putting it on top of all the other cases I already have and I am spent for the next several months. A lot of people are counting on me. When this case is all over, it will get better!"

Abigail stares at him for a second like he has grown two heads. "No, Lucas, it won't get better until you make it a priority for it to get better. You are always going to have more clients and more important cases! You must choose to put your family first! You could delegate some of these cases to other associates, I keep telling you about the same things over and over! You are choosing to be overworked!"

Lucas's phone begins to ring. He looks at it and looks back to Abigail before he starts to answer the call.

"Are you kidding me right now? This is exactly what I am talking about!" She throws her hands in the air, visibly frustrated.

"What? I have to answer it; it is for *work*. Do you really think that I would rather stand here and argue with you?"

Angry and exasperated, she looks at him as he starts to walk to his office before turning her back and storming out of the living room toward the backyard and her friends.

Lucas flinches as the back door slams behind him. "I am going to pay for this later," he thinks to himself as he answers the phone ringing in his hand.

Abigail makes her way out to the backyard and sees Allison and Benjamin sitting together on one of the lounge chairs. Benjamin has his hands tangled into Allison's hair while her arms wrap around his neck; they get lost in a passionate kiss. Hearing the door slam, Allison breaks the kiss and looks sadly at her friend, patting the chair next to her and Benjamin.

"Hey, girl, you, okay?" Allison asks quietly.

"I am so sorry you had to witness that," she says, embarrassed.

"It's fine; it was not awkward at all," she laughs.

"I will give you two lovely ladies some girl time. I'll meet you back in the house in a little bit," Benjamin says, rising off the chair and turning toward Allison. He gives her a quick peck on the lips and then turns to Abigail rubbing her arm. "It will be okay; he is just super stressed."

"Thanks, Ben," she smiles back as she sits next to her friend. Allison bumps her knee against Abigail's and raises her eyebrows waiting for her to say something.

"I just don't even know who he is anymore. He is always glued to his phone. He doesn't pay attention to anything any of us say or do; it's like he is not even here. I am just so frustrated, tired, and honestly, I am mentally exhausted," Abigail answers sadly.

"Seems like you two are fighting more and more these days. Have you thought about counseling?" She asks, concerned.

"I tried. Trust me, he refuses. He says he isn't going to pay someone to tell him everything he is doing wrong. He thinks counselors always just side with the wife anyway. I honestly don't know what to do anymore. I can't imagine living my life this way forever. If only we could go back in time," Abigail says while beginning to get lost in her thoughts.

"Remember the first night you guys met? You started texting me as soon as you got home. What was it, like three in the morning? Talking about how you met 'the one.' I told you that you were crazy. But you were right, Abby. You met your soulmate. Don't give up."

Abigail gazes off into the night and begins reminiscing about the night that she met Lucas and the life that they had built together over the last twenty years.

*Twenty years earlier- Abigail dances in the middle of the dance floor surrounded by a group of her friends when a handsome guy at the bar catches her eye. She stares entranced for a few minutes until he walks up to her and asks her name.*

*Abigail and Lucas spend the rest of the evening together, sharing phone numbers and making plans to get together the next day.*

*After that first evening, they spent almost every day at some point together. If they could not be together, they were on the phone or texting each other. Their friends considered them a fairy tale love at first sight couple.*

*Just a short eight months later, Lucas was sitting at a hibachi table at a Japanese Steakhouse rubbing his hands on the outside of his pants, trying to dry to sweat his hands kept accumulating. Finally, after their meal was over, he pushed out his chair and got down on one knee. You could hear a collective gasp from all of the women throughout the restaurant as they realized what was about to take place. Abigail knew from the moment her eyes met Lucas's that he would be the one she spent the rest of her life with, so it was a resounding yes that she happily screamed as he slipped a gorgeous ring onto her finger.*

*Flowers in her hair and sand in between her toes, a year later, Abigail was looking down an aisle on the beach at her groom. Surrounded by all of their friends and family, they became one. They were filled with love and all the hopes and dreams of a newlywed couple as they set off to create a beautiful life together. For so many years, it was.*

Breaking out of her daze, she glances at Allison, who is snapping her fingers in front of her face, trying to get her attention. They sit together in silence for a few minutes, unsure of what to say.

"You know I am always here if you want to talk, right?" Allison questions with a caring look in her eyes, breaking the silence.

"I know. It is stupid, really. He is a good man. He does take incredible care of us. He doesn't cheat. The kids and I do not want for anything. Except, I want to feel loved like I used to. I wish I could get his attention and feel important, like I am his everything. The way he made me feel before he became a highly sought-after criminal defense attorney. You know what I mean?" Abigail whispers sadly.

"Your feelings are not stupid, Abigail. Everyone wants to feel loved and desired," Allison says defensively.

The two sit quietly for a minute, and then Allison turns to Abigail with an idea.

"What if you guys went away for a mini-vacation? Take the kids out of school a few days early. Just get out of the house and enjoy some family time away from here."

"That sounds amazing, honestly, but he is so busy, I doubt he would even go."

"Make him go! It will be good for him too. I am sure the criminals can get by without him for one long weekend!" Allison states firmly.

"It really would be nice to get away; I will try to convince him!" Abigail nods in agreement. "Thanks for listening, you are a really good friend."

"Always and forever."

"Always and forever," Abigail repeats as she stands, hugging her best friend and walking with her, side by side, back into the house.

"Hey baby, you ready to go home?" Allison calls into the house to Benjamin.

He stands up from the couch and walks over to the women, grabbing hold of his wife's hand and kissing her cheek. "Ready whenever you are, my love. Abigail, you, okay?"

Smiling, she nods and walks them toward the front door. "I will be. Thanks for coming tonight, you guys. Sorry it turned out the way it did."

"Don't worry about it; if you need anything, you know where we are!" Allison responds quickly, assuring her friend as she and Benjamin walk out the front door to go back home. "I will call you in the morning to check on you."

"Goodnight, you guys," Abigail says as she closes the front door and lets out a long sigh.

Abigail stands against the closed front door, lost in her thoughts, pondering what her friend said. If she could convince Lucas to go away for a long weekend, it could be precisely what they need to get their family back on track—daydreaming about what kind of vacation they could take as she walks into her bedroom. Then, snapping back to reality when she sees Lucas come walking out of the closet, dressed in only pajama pants. Abigail is momentarily distracted by his toned, muscular chest. Her eyes travel down his chest and stop at his deep v sitting just above his pant line. She lets out a highly attracted sigh and looks up into her husband's eyes as he walks toward her.

Noticing his wife checking him out, he recognizes this as his chance to smooth things over. Looking at his wife apologetically, Lucas grabs hold of her arms gently and begins to whisper, "Listen, Abigail, about earlier," he starts.

"I know, me too," she responds, reaching for his waist and pulling him close. The touch of his skin on her hands sends goosebumps over her entire body. She shakes her head to clear out the thoughts she is currently having and refocus on what she wants to ask. "Lucas, I was thinking. What if we went away for a long weekend? Had some family time, away from here."

"You know I have this new case. I can't just go off on vacation when someone has hired me to defend their son for something so serious, Abigail," he says, trying to fight the frustration he feels beginning to surface.

"Listen, babe, just hear me out for a minute. I am only asking for a long weekend. You can't keep working nonstop. It isn't good for you or your family. It isn't healthy or normal. The stress you are putting on yourself is going to give you a heart attack," she pleads.

Taking his hands off her arms and running them through his hair, he lets out a sigh. "Abigail, seriously, please do not start this again. I *have* to work. I have people's lives in my hands, and they are depending on me."

Abigail closes the gap between them and places her hands gently on his cheeks while speaking softly, "Lucas, look at me. *We* depend on you too. We want you to be with us. Not just physically in the house, but actually present with us! Just one weekend. *Please,* Lucas, I am begging you. We all really need this."

He looks down into his wife's pleading eyes and knows that she is hurting. "*If only she could understand the stress I am under. Maybe she is right; maybe a little time away could be nice,*" he concludes to himself.

"Where would we even go?" He asks slowly as not to give her too much hope.

"I promise I will take care of everything! I will handle all the planning and packing; all you will have to do is get in the car when it is time to go. Just please say we can all go together."

Lucas, looking back into her pleading eyes, doesn't have the heart to tell her no. Deep down, he knows that this is a good idea for all of them.

"Okay, here is the deal. I will need at least a week before we leave so that I can meet with this new client and start to get things underway. I can only be gone for a maximum of 4 days. I will have to put in some work while we are gone, but I suppose it wouldn't hurt to get away for a few days. I will have my phone and laptop; if there is an emergency, people will still be able to get a hold of me. If you can agree to all of this, then I say okay, let's do it."

Abigail lets out a sigh of relief and wraps her arms around his neck. Lucas grabs her by the waist and squeezes, causing Abigail to let out a squeal. She pulls her husband down into a kiss. As the kiss deepens, Lucas grips her by the butt, lifting her in the air. Wrapping her legs around his waist and pulling him impossibly closer, she lets all of her anger from earlier in the evening dissipate. Filled with longing and hope, she puts all her love into that kiss. As he lays her gently onto the bed, a wave of pure happiness washes over her, and blissful memories play in her mind. Staring up at his bare muscular chest, she licks her lips in anticipation. He smiles down at her, recognizing her need. As he nuzzles her neck, he whispers, "I love you, Abigail."

Arching her back as he moves lower on her body, continuing to kiss her gently. "I love you too." They spend the next hour intertwined in each other's bodies, feeling nothing but pleasure as they make love, connecting with each other, and forgetting about their earlier argument.

The following day, Abigail wakes up with her head resting on Lucas's bare chest. "Good morning, beautiful." Lucas yawns as he wriggles to get out from underneath her. He kisses the top of her head and makes his way to the bathroom. "I have to go meet with that client at the jail this morning. It will be several hours before I get back home," he calls out as he starts the shower.

"But it is a Saturday," she whines back, slightly annoyed. The feelings of frustration from the day before threatening to seep back into her mind, but she pushes them away with the reminder that he had agreed to go away with the family. He must get this work out of the way first.

"What are you going to do today?" he asks, coming out of the bathroom dripping wet, wrapped with just a towel dangling dangerously low on his waist.

"Hot damn," Abigail jokes while eyeing her handsome husband. "Give me a shake."

Lucas turns around and shakes his butt at her while allowing the towel to fall. "OW!" she hollers, taking in the view. "I have to go pick up the kids, then I will start planning our getaway."

He looks at her as he gets dressed, considering asking her to cancel. But he notices the gleam in her eye and hates to disappoint her. "Just remember, I still have to work. This case is going to keep me very busy; you are going to have to just deal with that."

Rolling her eyes, she feels her anger rising back to the surface. "Deal with it? Seriously? How very kind of you. I am sure I will just deal with it." Getting up and walking into the bathroom, she slams the door ignoring Lucas's glare.

"Here we go again; I have to freaking work," Lucas mutters to himself as he finishes getting ready and heads out the door.

# CHAPTER 2

"Good morning, Brian," Lucas says, greeting the guard as he walks into the jail. "I am here to see a new client, Michael Huntsman."

"Geez, man, do you ever take a day off?" The guard laughs as Lucas walks through the metal detectors. "Go into room two, and I will have someone bring him in for you shortly."

"Thanks, buddy. Tell Lacey I said hi. We should get together for dinner again soon!" Lucas replies, walking down the hall. Once he steps into room number two, he pops open his briefcase, pulling out a notepad and placing it on the table in front of him. Hearing the door creak open, he turns to greet his new client. The man standing in front of him is not at all who he imagined.

"Michael Huntsman?"

"Were you expecting someone else?"

"No, just making sure," he responds slowly.

Lucas eyes the young man carefully. He couldn't be more than eighteen. His parents said he was a kid, but they all say that even when they are in their forties. Not realizing they are enabling them with their babying. This time, they were actually telling the truth; this client is a kid. He looks like he should be walking the halls of some prep school, not shackled, walking into a jail interview room. The inmate was of average height, muscular build, and boyish good looks. His eyes were red and puffy from crying. How could this clean-cut teen be in here on charges of murder?

Michael sits down at the table across from Lucas, not making a sound. Instead, he stares back with his bloodshot eyes.

"Is anyone bothering you in here, son?"

"No," was his short answer reply.

"Now is the time to be honest, if there is anyone hurting you let me know! I can put in a request to get your cell changed."

"No one is doing anything to me, but even if they were, I would deserve it."

"What do you mean? Why would you say that?" Lucas questions warily.

"Do you even know why I am in here?" Michael snarls.

"Well, I spoke with your parents last night, and they have retained me to represent you in your pending criminal case. I have read the charges but am unclear of the facts in the case. Would you mind telling me what happened in your own words?" Lucas asks as he pulls his notepad in front of him and lifts his pen.

"I told them I do not want an attorney. However, I am willing to take the punishment for what I did."

"Why not? You don't want to go into court without someone fighting for you on your side, trust me," Lucas continues.

"I haven't talked to anyone about it. I don't want to talk about it. I *don't* want your help. I deserve whatever I have coming to me. Just leave me alone."

Lucas looks at him for a moment, unsure of what to say. Then, finally, he lets out a long sigh and begins. "It would really make more sense to me why you feel that way if you would tell me your version of what happened. Your parents were fairly vague on your case, wanting you to fill me in on the details. I want to help you, and not to brag, but I am very good at what I do. So, help me, help you. What happened that night?"

Michael looks back at Lucas and slowly shakes his head. "I don't deserve help; no one should be arguing on my behalf. She would be here if it weren't for me."

Lucas stares on, allowing his eyes to beg Michael to continue. Then, as a tear forms in the corner of his eye, he hung his head and pressed on.

"Fine, when I am done, you will understand, and you will realize why you shouldn't bother with me. We went to a house party after the football game. We had won, and all of us were riled up and ready to let off some steam. Lydia, my girlfriend, and I stayed at the party for several hours. Her curfew was coming up, so I needed to get her home. She had more to drink than I had; I felt fine. I thought I was fine, turns out I wasn't," Michael whispered before he let out a small sob.

"It's okay; take your time."

"You don't understand; it is never going to be okay. She is dead because of me."

Lucas nodded slowly, put his hand on top of Michael's and patted him gently. "What happened next?"

"Lydia was chatting away in the passenger seat, making plans for our future. I started to feel a little bit lightheaded and the lines in the road were becoming just slightly blurry. She asked me several times if I was okay, I think she was getting worried as I crossed the center line once or twice. I knew we were not too far away and was confident that I could get us to her house safely. My plan was to just crash in my truck until the alcohol wore off, then I would head home. I got a text from my buddy asking about going to the gym the next morning. I grabbed the phone and was sending him a quick reply. Lydia was yelling at me to put the phone down, I didn't realize it, but I had drifted off the road. It was too late to correct. We went down the embankment, and my truck rolled. She was pinned. I couldn't get her out. She was screaming for my help. I tried, I tried." Michael was bawling, crying at this point.

With tears streaming down his face, Michael looked up at Lucas. "You see, I don't deserve your help. I killed Lydia."

Lucas sat quietly for a moment with his hand on top of Michael's so that he could regulate his breathing and clear his thoughts. Then, once he was in control of his emotions, he looked over to Michael with sympathy and began speaking to him again.

"Michael, everyone deserves help. I am so sorry that happened to you and your girlfriend. I cannot even imagine the pain that you are in right now. You made some bad choices, and you are going to have to live with those choices for the rest of your life. I am going to be honest with you though, you are facing some serious charges and looking at up to 25 years in prison."

Michael nodded his head in understanding and looked down at his hands as he played with his fingers.

"Have you or your parents talked to Lydia's family?"

"They came by and saw me while I was in the hospital. The hurt and anguish on their faces I will never get out of my head."

"I wouldn't wish that pain on anyone, their statement will go a long way in the punishment of this case though, so I am going to have to follow up with them too. Is there anything you would like me to relay to them on your behalf?" Lucas asks solemnly.

"Just tell them that I am so sorry, I would do anything to switch places with her. I wish it was me and not her. I loved her so much," Michael chokes out before placing his head back into his hands in anguish.

"I will get ahold of the state's evidence and see about getting you out of here on bond. Then, I am going to talk to your parents and make sure they get you into a counseling program. You are going to need someone to help you work through all of the emotional stuff that comes with what happened."

Michael just nods and wipes his fingers along the brim of his nose.

"I will call your parents on my way out of here and give them an update. I will try to come back in and see you in a few days as well."

Lucas stands up and motions for the guard to open the door. Then, turning back to Michael, he places his hand on his shoulder and gives it a slight squeeze before walking out.

*"An innocent girl is now gone, her poor parents. If that Lydia was my Madison, I don't know how I could go on. Kids just don't think about consequences. Should he spend 25 years in prison for his stupid choices, though?"* Lucas wrestles with his thoughts as he walks towards his car.

Driving home, Lucas calls Michael's parents and fills them in on how the meeting went at the jail with their son.

"Good morning, Mr. Huntsman, I wanted to touch base with you. I just left the jail from visiting Michael; after some coaxing, I was able to get him to give me his version of what occurred that night. I must tell you his case is a tragedy. I highly recommend you get him into counseling to deal with the death of Lydia and the stress of the criminal case immediately. I would also recommend you and your wife go and visit him as often as possible until he is released. I am going to work with the prosecutor and the judge on Monday to get him out on bond so he will at least be back at home while we work through the stages of this case. He shouldn't be stuck in the jail; he isn't a threat to society."

"Thank you so much, Mr. Ferguson. Please do whatever you can; you must help him. He is just a child," the father pleads.

"I will do my best, but Michael is going to be punishing himself for a long time as well. He is going to need serious counseling to help with that," Lucas replies honestly. "I picked up the police report and will go over it tonight."

"We trust you; everyone knows that you are the best attorney in town. Whatever you need his mother and I to do, just let me know."

"I will keep in touch." Lucas says with a sigh while hanging up the phone, exasperated as he pulls into the driveway of his home. He sits and stares at his house, thinking about his kids for a few minutes before exiting his car and going inside.

The moment he walks in the front door, he smells cinnamon rolls baking in the kitchen and can hear the chatter of his kids throughout the house.

"Daddy, Daddy, guess what I did at Crystal's house?" Kaitlyn exclaims with excitement, running to her father and wrapping her arms around his leg happily.

"Daddy has a lot of work to do, honey. Tell me about it a little bit later, okay?" he replies, pinching the bridge of his nose and wriggling out of her grasp, heading towards his home office. She has a visible frown on her face as she watches him walk away.

"That was rude!" Abigail snaps, following her husband into his office. "She was excited to tell you about her night and you totally blew her off! She is just a child, *your* child."

"Oh my gosh, Abigail, stop it! I am busy. I told her I would talk to her about it later!" he yells back angrily, flinging his briefcase onto his desk.

"This is exactly what I was saying to you last night! You always put us last. Why does your work come have to come before all of us?"

"Are we seriously going to do this again right now? I have a lot of information to go over. It is time-sensitive and extremely important. The life of a young man has been placed in my hands."

"Whatever, Lucas, nice priorities," Abigail mutters as she angrily walks away.

Walking throughout the house looking for her children, she finds them playing on the swing set in the backyard. Madison pushes Brody on the swing while Kaitlyn sits at the top of the slide, chatting cheerfully about her sleepover to her siblings, who were only half paying attention.

"Hey, kiddos. I am glad you are all home, I missed all of you, it is so empty in the house when you are all gone at the same time. What would you guys like to have for lunch?" Abigail asks, sitting next to Brody on the empty swing. "I am making your favorite cinnamon rolls for dessert!"

"Pizza!" Brody hollers, kicking his legs excitedly. "And then yummy cinnamon rolls."

"Pizza it is then!" she replies, standing up from the swing and taking a step back toward the house.

"Mommy, are you and Daddy going to get a divorce?" Kaitlyn asks quietly.

Abigail stops quickly and spins around facing her children, a look of shock spread across her face.

"What? No, of course not. Why would you ask such a thing, honey?"

"I heard you and Daddy fighting again," she responds sadly. "I didn't mean to make you guys' fight, I just wanted to tell daddy about what I did last night."

"Oh baby, you did not make us fight, please don't ever think that! Sometimes mommy's and daddy's just fight, it has nothing to do with you I promise!" Abigail said as she rushed to the edge of the slide placing her hand on Kaitlyn's leg lovingly.

"My friend, Max's parents are divorced so he has two houses, and two Christmases and two birthdays. But he said his parents still fight all the time," Brody states matter-of-factly.

"We are not getting divorced; we just had an argument.

Daddy is really busy with work and just took on a big new case and is very stressed."

"Daddy never plays with me anymore," Brody sighs.

"I'm sorry, baby. It will get better. I was going to save it for a surprise, but we are all going to go away on a mini family vacation next weekend!"

"Whoo-hoo, vacation!" Kaitlyn exclaims, sliding down the slide while pumping her arms in the air happily.

"But, Mom, what about Tony?"

"Madison, you can go a few days without seeing your boyfriend. We are going to enjoy some much needed family time."

"Ugh, that's not fair; it's not like Dad is going to spend any time with us anyway," she whines back.

"Stop it right now, young lady."

"Well, can he at least come over for dinner tonight?"

"If you can change your attitude, Tony is welcome to join us later on for dinner," Abigail states sternly. "Now, you guys can play for a little bit longer, I will go order the pizza and finish up the planning for our trip."

Later that evening, the family, joined by Tony in the dining room, ate dinner and chatted happily. Everyone except Lucas, of course. He spent his time in between bites typing away on his cell phone. Abigail said nothing, deciding she did not have the energy to argue with him again tonight.

# CHAPTER 3

The following Thursday, Abigail and the kids are loading up the car for their trip early in the morning. Abigail leans back from the trunk and yells towards the house in frustration.

"Lucas, Lucas! We are ready to go."

"Okay, I need just five more minutes," he hollers back from inside.

"Uggggh, that is what he always says. We are never going to get out of here!" Kaitlyn whines.

"Now, Kaitlyn, let's try to be patient with Daddy for just a few more minutes. He is trying to get everything situated with work so we can have this family time together," Abigail says soothingly.

"I'll try, Mommy. I am just so excited."

"I know, baby, me too. Does anyone have to go to the bathroom before we get on the road?" Abigail questions, closing the trunk and looking around to make sure everything is ready.

"Mom, seriously. We aren't babies. We know when we have to go to the bathroom," Madison says as she rolls her teenage eyes in annoyance and slips into the backseat of the car, putting in her earbuds.

"Lucas, honey, please. The kids are waiting, and it has been almost twenty minutes since the last time you asked for five more minutes," Abigail pleads.

"Well, I wasn't the one that planned a weekend getaway at the last minute, in the middle of me trying to save a kid from spending half of his life in prison," Lucas sarcastically says as he walks toward the car while texting anxiously.

"Seriously? We haven't even left the driveway. Can you please just put that away for a little while?" Abigail complains while Lucas texts from the driver's seat.

Lucas looks over at her slowly and stares with a stern gaze.

"Are you going to nag me the entire trip?"

"Well, that depends. Are you only going to work and continue to ignore us the entire trip?" she replies while shrugging her shoulders.

Lucas glares back at his wife, who holds his gaze until he drops his phone into his lap and begins to pull out of the driveway.

"Thank you." She whispers while crossing her arms across her chest.

After driving in silence for a few hours, Abigail turns to look at her children in the back seat; all of them are sound asleep. Next, she glances over to her husband, who has his attention focused on the road, before turning her face to gaze out the window at the gorgeous mountainous scenery surrounding her.

"Lucas, how did we get here?" Abigail questions quietly.

"What do you mean? You're the one that put the address in the GPS; I am just following the directions," he replies, looking at her in a panic. "Are we lost?"

Rolling her eyes and letting out a frustrated sigh, she tries to correct herself to make him understand. "That is not what I meant, Lucas. I mean how did *we* get here?" she asks while motioning between the two of them. "I really want this weekend to get our relationship back on track. We are falling apart at the seams, and you either don't notice or just don't care. Either way, the train is derailing, and it's derailing fast."

Lucas reaches over for Abigail's hand and squeezes it gently.

"Abby, you know that I love you, but you have to calm down. You are always nagging me and whining about the dumbest stuff. I am busy. Sometimes I just want to scream, 'Get off my nuts.' You are expecting way too much from me right now, and I can't give it to you. I do not mean to make you feel less important than you are; however, I need you to stop trying to micromanage me or handle me like one of the kids," he says reassuringly.

Abigail turns in her seat to face him as she pulls her hand away and stares in silence for a few seconds before slowly speaking.

"I am sorry that I *nag* you about spending time with your family. You know what would be amazing, Lucas? If you would actually do it on your own because you want to! Do you think it makes me feel good to have to constantly beg my own husband for attention and time away from his work and freaking phone? It isn't just your life anymore, Lucas. It's *our* life! And it has been for a long time. It's past time that you realized that and got with the program." she explains, exasperated.

"Is this entire trip going to be this way? I seriously could have just stayed home and worked and done without you wanting to fight with me all the time! I was trying to tell you to relax and that we are going to be alright. You somehow twisted it into something completely different and not anything close to what I meant," he says, annoyed.

Abigail reaches over with both of her hands, grabbing ahold of Lucas's free hand, and cups it close to her body.

"Lucas, I know the deal we agreed to, but you have to hold

up your end too. I will try to back off some, but you have to put in the effort with us also. *Please*, try and enjoy this weekend with us. You just don't seem to know how much we all need this time together."

"I will try to spend as much time this weekend as I can focusing on you and the kids and not on work. However, you must understand that I can't just ignore work altogether."

"Thank you! I do understand, and when you need to get work done, I will make an honest effort to leave you alone about it!" she nods happily.

Lucas pulls one of her hands to his lips and kisses the top before letting go of her hand and putting his on her upper thigh.

"*I think Allison may have been right about this,*" Abigail thinks to herself happily.

A short time later, the family arrives at their destination—a massive, gorgeous log cabin surrounded by Tennessee's beautiful woods and mountains.

"Who would have thought such beautiful scenery was just a few hours from our house?" Lucas mused, looking around and taking a deep breath of the fresh, clean air. The wind rustling in the trees causing a calming effect upon the father.

The kids hopped out of the car and ran onto the porch chasing after each other in a game of tag.

"You're it!" Madison yells as she tags Brody.

"No fair, you are the fastest," he whines back.

"Come on, you know you are fast. Go get Kaitlyn!" She laughs back. "Mom, can we go inside now?"

Abigail and Lucas grab a couple of bags from the car and head toward the front door. When they open it, they all gasp with delight. The owner of this rental cabin spared no expense in designing and decorating it. Windows covered the entire back of the house facing the mountains. The warm and inviting living room would make anyone feel completely at home.

"This place is amazing!" Madison says as the kids come through the front door behind their parents.

"Can we live here?" Brody asks, eyes wide in wonder.

"No, stupid, we can't live here! What about Tony? Your friends? School?" Madison replies in her teenage, annoyed voice.

"Madison, be nice. No name-calling," Abigail scolds. "I swear, one minute she is being sweet and playing with her brother and sister and the next she acts like she can't stand them, teenage mood swings are really a lot," she continued under her breath walking toward the back porch.

"Look at this hot tub, it is huge!" Kaitlyn exclaims as she points at the large eight- seater hot tub sitting on the back porch in front of a huge picture window.

"I wanna go in the hot tub, mom, can we?" Brody asks with wide pleading eyes.

"Of course, baby, we will spend plenty of time in the hot tub, but not right now. Let's get settled in first, okay?" Abigail replied with a smile.

As they all walk throughout the cabin, getting acquainted with their home for the next couple of days, the mood is light, and everyone is happy.

"It really is beautiful, honey. This was a good idea. I can literally feel the stress leaving my body by the second," Lucas states as he walks up behind Abigail grabbing her by the waist, pulling her in close and kissing the top of her head.

"You have no idea how happy that makes me, babe," she replies, turning into his embrace and leaning in for a passionate kiss.

After she pulls her lips away from the kiss, she remains snuggled in his arms. Stepping back and looking up at him with a light in her eyes she smiles and nudges him with her shoulder gently.

"You looked stressed," she whispered rubbing her hand along his cheek softly.

"It has been a rough couple of months," he replied leaning into her hand and turning his face to kiss her fingers lightly.

Watching his face, she sees the weight of the world on his shoulders reflecting in his eyes and realizes that she is a part of that. If only he didn't work so hard, he could enjoy his life more.

" I have an idea; let's all go for a walk into town before we finish settling in. We can see what they have down there, grab a bite to eat, and enjoy the nature and fresh air before it gets too dark."

"I think that sounds like a great plan, let me just check my email really quick," Lucas replies, grabbing his cell phone out of his pocket.

"Why don't you guys run to the bathroom really quick before we head out?" Abigail asks pointing to the kids.

Madison rolls her eyes and cocks an eyebrow at her mother in annoyance while Kaitlyn and Brody skip off toward the bathroom.

"Seriously, why do you act like I am a baby? When I have to go pee, I will pee, I do not need any reminders! And why are we walking into town when we have a perfectly good car that can drive us there?" She asks with the attitude only a teenager could muster.

Abigail takes a deep breath and then lets out a frustrated sigh, counting to three in her head before answering.

"Madison, honey, we are going to be walking so we can enjoy the outdoors and get out of the car we have been sitting in for the last several hours. As for the bathroom it was just a random suggestion since we are going to be walking for a while and I didn't want you to have to pee behind a tree."

"Whatever Mom," Madison replies putting her air pods in her ears and tuning her mother out.

Abigail looks back in surprise and ponders what happened

to the little girl who used to cling to her and dote on her every word. How did she become someone her daughter found to be so annoying? "I don't care so much for this version of my little girl," she mutters to herself as she turns toward Lucas ready to vent but stops short when she notices he too looks aggravated as he smacks his cell phone willing it to work.

"There is no reception here. Are you serious? So, we are literally in a place where I couldn't work for five minutes if I had to! We had an agreement, Abigail; I must have access to my clients. Did you pick this place on purpose? So that I couldn't work?"

"Don't be ridiculous, you know me better than that, I would never do such a thing. I picked this place because it was beautiful and had good reviews and was a place we could get away and relax!" She snapped back in frustration.

"So, it just happens to be a fantastic coincidence for you, that the place you picked for us to relax forces me to not work even though the only reason I consented to this trip was because you assured me, I could still get stuff done?"

"Lucas, calm down; we are in the middle of the woods. I am sure once we get into town, there will be reception, and you can check your email and get whatever you need to do done before we head back up here to the cabin," Abigail says while rubbing her hand along his arm reassuringly to relax him.

Lucas shoves his phone back into his pocket out of sheer frustration and heads toward the front door flinging it open and stepping out onto the front porch.

"Kids lets go," he shouts back over his shoulder as he notices a large basket at the corner of the porch overflowing with balls and outdoor toys.

He walks over to the basket, reaches in, and pulls out a football. Tossing the ball back and forth between his hands, he reminisces about his younger years when he was his high school's football team's captain. Back when his most significant stress was beating the rival high school on a Friday night.

While he was remembering his past Abigail and the kids had walked out of the cabin and were walking down the porch steps. Lucas hearing their chatter was brought out of his daze and tossed the ball towards his son.

"Hey Brody, think fast," he shouted as the ball began hurtling toward the surprised youngster.

However, Brody was caught off guard and was not prepared to catch the ball, allowing it to smack him right in the face. He let out an ear-piercing cry and dropped to his knees on the ground sobbing.

"What is the world is wrong with you?" Madison shouted as she cradled Brody in her arms.

"What? I thought he would catch it." Lucas said defensively while shrugging his shoulders.

Abigail came running up behind the kids sliding down onto the ground in front of Brody grabbing his face and examining it closely. There was a small red bump and a trickle of blood on the corner of his nose that she quickly wiped off with her thumb and then rubbed off her finger onto the bottom of her shorts.

"You seriously hit him in the face with a football!" She yelled while holding Brody close to her chest.

Lucas looked back at them in shock and threw his hands up in defense. "*Obviously* I did NOT mean to hit him in the face, I was just trying to toss the football to my son. I thought he would catch it!"

"Have you ever played football with Brody dad? He hates football!" Madison shouted flinging her arms at him angrily.

"How can he hate football? I was a star football player," Lucas asks confusion written all over his face as he walks down the porch steps toward his family.

Brody stood up with Abigail and as Lucas came closer, he pressed his face into her stomach turning away from his father.

"Newsflash dad, not everything is about you. Just because you played football doesn't mean Brody will."

"Brody, buddy I am sorry, I didn't mean to hit you. I really did think you would catch it."

"He is just a little boy Lucas, even if he did like football his coordination is nowhere near where it needs to be for you to just absentmindedly throw a ball at his face," Abigail scolds while rubbing the youngsters back.

"Good grief, I get it okay. I said I was sorry; can we just drop it now and get going into town?" Lucas asks as he pushes past his family and heads off toward the trail leading them into town through the lush green woods.

Madison rolls her eyes and follows behind with Abigail, Brody, and Kaitlyn. "Gee this should be fun, not," she mumbles to herself.

"Are you okay Brody?" Kaitlyn questions with worry lacing her voice as she walked behind him.

"Mmmhmm," he mumbled in response as he pulled his head off his mother's side, realizing he had gotten a tiny amount of blood on her shirt.

"Sorry, mommy."

Looking down at where Brody was staring with a look of panic on his face, Abigail shrugged her shoulders and gave him a small hug.

"It's okay buddy, it's just a shirt, let's get going.

The family walks along the trail, chatting amongst themselves for about thirty minutes before reaching the edge of town. Stopping to stare at the scene before them, they stand with their mouths agape. Cranston Creek was a quaint little town featuring brick-lined streets and large older but well-kept buildings. As they take a moment to soak it all in, the adults realize that it doesn't look like it has changed much since the 1950s. While the architecture of the buildings looks to be from a different era, they have been very well maintained, and almost all of them look nearly new —all except for one lone building on the end of the street.

As they look around, they watch as children walk by holding balloons, and families mingle together happily. The atmosphere all around is cheerful and light.

"Look how adorable this place is!" Abigail exclaims, looking around in awe. "This quite possibly by the cutest town I have ever seen in my entire life!"

"It's pretty cute, I just hope that my freaking phone will work down here!" Lucas grumbles.

"Are you two serious? This is absolutely the creepiest place I have ever seen!" Madison exclaims looking back at her parents dumbfounded.

"Lucas, please. Just relax, you are going to be able to check in soon. I promise, and Madison, what in the world are you talking about? What would make you say such a thing?" Abigail questions as she looks at her daughter like she just grew and extra head.

"Ummm, every scary movie ever! Normal people are not this happy, let alone an entire town! Look around, this place is weird. I mean it, we need to go back up to that cabin and get the heck out of here."

"Oh, for Pete's sake Madison, get a grip, we are not leaving. You can knock it off right now. I know you just want to get back home to Tony. Trust me, he will still be there next week!" Abigail states in frustration.

"This has nothing to do with Tony, but whatever, if some weirdo starts chasing us with a chainsaw or something I will use my last breath to say I told you so."

"Madison, stop being so dramatic, the south is known for being more friendly than most other places," Lucas grumbles annoyed.

"I think it looks nice," Kaitlyn says grabbing a hold of her father's hand with a smile.

As the family walks down the street, people-watching, and window shopping through the shops as they pass by, an older woman with a strong southern accent and a giant smile greets them.

"Hey there, y'all. My name is Barbara. Welcome to Cranston Creek. Is this your first time visiting? Where are y'all staying? Where are y'all from?" she questions cheerfully.

"Why, thank you. How kind. Yes, this is our first time visiting. I absolutely love your town! We are renting the Bibler cabin, right up the ridge for a few days," Abigail responds while turning to point in the direction from which they just came.

"Ah, that is a beautiful place. Gorgeous views! Make sure you and the kiddos watch out for bears, though!" Barbara cautions with a smile.

"*Bears*! There are bears?" Brody squeals in fear.

"Why sure, honey. You are staying smack dab in the middle of their front yard. These woods are filled with all kinds of animals. Beautiful creatures. But don't you worry, kiddo. You don't bother them, and they won't bother you. Just don't be leaving any food outside now!" She responds with a chuckle.

The children look at their parents with fear, and Abigail smiles warmly back at them, nodding in reassurance.

"No worries, we will be very careful and keep an eye out for them. We won't leave out any trash or food."

"I don't want to see any bears mommy; they won't go up to the hot tub, will they?" Kaitlyn asks concerned.

"No honey, they won't go up to the hot tub, but we will watch out for them just in case, okay?" Abigail responds reassuringly.

Kaitlyn looks back at her mother unsure but nods her head in understanding anyway. Hopeful that her mother was right.

Lucas, looking at his phone, tapping on the screen in irritation, interrupts the conversation.

"Sorry to interrupt but, do you know where I can get onto Wi-Fi around here? I really need to check into work. Knowing everything is okay at the office will allow me to try and relax with my family on this little vacation, and I am having a really hard time getting anything to load."

"*Maybe he really is going to try, this might actually work,*" Abigail thinks to herself as Barbara smiles back at him sweetly.

"Of course, honey; we aren't barbaric. While up at your cabin and even here in town service can be rather spotty, all the shops here on the strip have Wi-Fi, and they are more than happy to let you use it!" She offers while looking over to the children with an idea. "You three make sure your parents take you to Mrs. Fran's candy shop. Guaranteed to give you the biggest sugar rush you have ever had."

Eyes wide with excitement, the kids look over at their mother, who chuckles back at their expressions.

"That does sound fun, we will be sure to check her store out. Also, where would be the best place to eat dinner?" Abigail asks, looking around at all the buildings on the street.

"Oh honey! When you are ready to eat real food, you have to go to MawMaw's Country Kitchen. You won't find better southern hospitality or down-home country cooking anywhere in the United States!" Barbara responds with assurance while pointing down the street toward the local diner.

"That sounds perfect and delicious, thank you!" Abigail replies.

"What is that?" Kaitlyn questions, looking across the street at the only run-down building around. You couldn't see inside from the road because the windows were blacked out. A flickering sign reads, "Mystical Magic Emporium."

"Oh darlin', that is Mr. John's place. It's an odd little shop to stop in for tourists. It is a little bit creepy, but if you like magic, it can be very entertaining," Barbara responded while shrugging her shoulders.

"Mommy, can we go there?" Brody asks, staring curiously at the building.

"I don't know, buddy," she responds warily.

"Daddy, please can we go?" Brody pleads with his father while tugging on his arm.

"Does it have Wi-Fi?" Lucas asks Barbara.

"Sure does," she responds, nodding and continuing to smile.

"Alright, bud, let's go!" Lucas states as he grabs Brody's hand and leads him across the street, with the rest of the family following closely behind.

"I wouldn't touch anything in there; I wouldn't want anyone to turn into a frog!" Barbara chuckles as the Ferguson family enters the store.

# CHAPTER 4

*O*nce inside, the children scoot closer to their mother as they look around at their surroundings. The dimly lit interior and strange, spooky music playing over the store's speakers gives off a scary vibe. The walls had been decorated in what looks like Halloween décor. All kinds of magic kits and props fill the shelves in between the dust that has settled in everywhere. The musty aroma causes Abigail to crinkle her nose in disgust.

"This is definitely not a whimsical fun type of magic shop," Abigail slowly says as she looks around the store and wraps an arm around Kaitlyn protectively.

"Why does it stink so bad?" Kaitlyn questions plugging her nose with her fingers and shaking her head.

"Well, this is not exactly what I was expecting," Lucas whispers.

"Okay, you guys, seriously, do not touch anything!" Abigail states firmly, trying to hide the hint of fear in her voice.

"This place is sooo cool!" Madison exclaims as she walks towards some items on a shelf nearby.

"Madison, get back here! Stay close." Abigail scolds.

"Ugggg, what do you think is going to happen to me? Good grief, mother, we are in a small store in a dinky little town," she responds, rolling her eyes and walking further down the aisle.

Lucas looks at Abigail and just shrugs before once again pulling out his phone.

"Good afternoon, folks. Welcome to Mystical Magical Emporium; my name is John. Is there anything I can help you with today?" A large man with a deep voice asks as he walks over toward the family.

The deep mysterious voice sends a shiver up Abigail's spine. She eyes him carefully, and her gut tells her that something is not right with this older gentleman. He was about six feet tall, wearing aged looking yet clean clothes with weathered and worn hands. As Abigail examined John, she guessed he was in his sixties based upon his silver hair. But the long deep scar that started at his temple and went down to the top of his lip was what caused her to pause and stare a minute. What would cause such a scar? A bar fight? Was he in the military? Is he dangerous? As all of these thoughts swirled around in her mind, she glanced at her husband, who was shaking his phone impatiently, utterly oblivious to the fear in Abigail's eyes.

John was fully aware of the intense stare coming from Abigail and smirked internally.

Lucas looked up to the stranger and nodded his head. "Yes, actually you could be of great help to me, does your store have Wi-Fi? I am having difficulty accessing anything on my phone and I need to check in on a few things at work?"

"Yes, sir, of course, the password is magic8," the shop owner replies with a smirk that gave Abigail the heebie-jeebies.

"Thank you!" Lucas replies as he begins to walk away, typing fervently onto his phone.

John turns to Abigail as she starts to walk down the aisle in an attempt to put distance between her and John. "Are your kids into magic?" He questions to her retreating form.

Brody spun around while holding onto Abigail's hand causing her to turn as well. Jumping up and down with excitement he exclaims, "I am! I wish I could do magic like Houdini!"

"Now those are some big shoes to fill little fella, but in all actuality, anyone can do magic! You just need the right tools, imagination, and the desire to be great," John replies while patting Brody on the head.

Brody looks up at his mother with wide excited eyes and began pleading. "Mommy, can we get a magic kit? Please? Pretty please, Mommy?"

"Let's look around a little bit first, honey, then we will see," she replies while ushering him along with his sister, hoping to finally put distance between them and John. She couldn't understand why, but he really gave her the creeps. Glancing over her shoulder she watches as he kept within a few feet of her and the kids and that made her even more comfortable.

"Why will this guy not take a hint?" She mumbles under her breath.

"So, your husband, he is a very busy man?" John questions following closely behind. They both turn to look at Lucas, who is typing onto his phone and mumbling to himself on the other side of the store, oblivious to anything else going on around him.

"Yes, he has a very important job and stays incredibly busy," she responds as she and the kids continue to walk away and look at other items.

John stares over at Lucas for a few minutes, watching him with interest before walking towards him. Lips drawn in a straight line and brows furrowed contemplating the character of the man before him. After standing next to him for a few minutes in silence he decided to broach a conversation.

"Hey there, sir. Everything okay?" John asks.

While focusing on something on his phone instead of his surroundings, Lucas does not realize that the shop owner is talking to him and ignores the question while continuing to work in silence.

"Sir, excuse me. Is everything okay? John repeats a little bit louder and with a bit more force, causing Lucas to look up startled.

"Oh, I apologize. I didn't realize you were talking to me. Yes, everything is fine. I am just getting a little bit of work done while my family looks around."

"I see. I don't have one of those so-called smartphones. Seems to me that they are making people dumb. Folks don't talk to each other anymore. I sure hate to see people with their face down just staring at those things. I refuse to let that be me. Disconnecting and not having actual conversations with real live individuals, no sir, not for me," John says, shaking his head disapprovingly.

"Well, if I didn't have one, I would be working fifty times more than I do now! They actually are a great tool for those of us in the professional world," Lucas, offended, responds rudely.

"Yeah, that is what the *'professional people'* keep telling me," John snaps back annoyed.

Lucas, putting his phone back into his pocket, looks at John perplexed. The two stare at each other for a few seconds in total silence before something moves and catches Lucas's eye. He points to a ridiculously odd-looking black hat with eight octopus-looking arms coming out of the top that move and sway on their own at random moments, almost as if the hat were alive.

"What in the world is that?" Lucas asks curiously as he walks slowly toward the counter where the hat was sitting atop a stand. Leaning toward it eyes wide filled with interest, he turns his head from side to side to look at all the angles he could from where the hat sat. It was such a peculiar hat; it was drawing him in, and it had his full attention.

"Well, this is a very powerful wizard hat. It's a one of a kind and holds many magical powers," John says slowly, lifting the hat off the stand, holding it in front of Lucas to examine more closely. "It has been in my family for generations, passed down from father to son and so on."

"As if that were a thing," Lucas laughs while watching the hat and its sporadic movements carefully. He could not take his eyes off the hat. Completely mesmerized by the hideous object.

"I can assure you, sir, this hat and its abilities are genuine, John replies sternly while carefully placing his hand atop the hat.

"Magic is for children; an illusion, it isn't something that is actually real, it is just for fun. So, is it battery powered or something?" He questions as he moves his head closer to the hat, examining the tentacles carefully.

"Try it on; you may be surprised," John states with a mischievous grin.

Lucas continues to stare at the hat for a minute, thinking. Then, looking back toward his family on the other side of the store, he catches Abigail's eye. She smiles at him warmly before turning her attention back to Brody, who is asking her a question. Satisfied that he will not have witnesses to what he is about to do, he reaches for the hat, taking it from John's hands, and placing it gently on top of his head.

"Do I look as stupid as I feel?" Lucas asks with a nervous laugh.

"Not at all. In fact, it fits you quite well, Mr. Ferguson," John replies with an evil gleam in his eye.

"Wait. What? How did you know my name?" Lucas asks, confused.

Lucas, looks over at John and is met with a sinister stare. Becoming super uncomfortable, he begins to reach up to take the hat off his head when he starts to feel extremely lightheaded. Reaching for the edge of the counter to steady himself as the room begins to spin, he attempts to turn around to alert Abigail that he desperately needs help, but his body will not cooperate. He looks up at John and the sinister stare he receives causes his stomach to drop right before he felt his body falling toward the floor with him having no ability to stop it.

"What in the—" Lucas attempts to say but is unable to finish his sentence before he crashes into a heap on the floor. Sweat pouring down his forehead while he struggled to breathe. He could vaguely see the outline of John through the black spots in his vision leaning down toward him before everything went black.

Meanwhile, on the other side of the store, Abigail is talking with the children.

"Mommy, can we get something, please? I really, really want to become a magician," Brody pleads with his mother.

"Well, that depends, are you going to turn creepy like that John guy?" Abigail laughs while looking around nervously hoping that he did not overhear her snide comment.

"No, I promise. But it will be so fun, we can play together and put on magic shows for you and daddy. You will love it!" He replies happily while Kaitlyn nods her head beside him in agreement.

"Okay, here is the deal, you guys can pick out one thing to share, but you have to all agree on whatever it is. I am going to go and get your dad and let him know that we are ready to go. You guys stay together and meet me at the register when you have picked out what you are getting."

"Deal!" Kaitlyn exclaims reaching for a box on the shelf eagerly.

"No, not that one," Brody argues reaching for the box next to the one Kaitlyn just picked up.

"Remember the rules, no fighting, and you have to all three agree."

"Yes mommy," Brody states while glaring at Kaitlyn.

Abigail nods to the children and then walks around the store quickly but is unable to find her husband. Going over to the register where her kids are waiting, she has a look of worry on her face. Lucas hates to wait at stores while she shops. She really did not want to have another argument on this trip. Brushing it off at the sight of her kids' excited expressions, she grabs for her wallet out of her purse and smiles.

"Mom, we all agreed on this one, no fighting!" Kaitlyn exclaims. "We will play together nicely, promise!"

"Okay! Sounds good to me. If you all agreed, we can get this one. Now, let's pay quickly and find Daddy. You know how he hates waiting," she responds while continuing to look around the store, unable to see her husband above any of the shelves.

"I will be with you guys in just one minute," John says as he bends over and picks up the hat Lucas had just been trying on a minute ago up off the floor.

"What in the world is that ugly thing?" Madison wonders aloud with a disgusted look on her face.

"Oh, this old thing? It is just for decoration. I have had this silly hat for years and years," John replies while placing the hat back onto its stand with care.

"I think it is time to throw it out," Madison mumbles.

"Madison, where are your manners? Good grief? I apologize, but I was wondering, did you happen to see where my husband went?" Abigail questions.

"No, ma'am. I'm sorry, I was not paying too much attention to your husband. He seemed preoccupied with his phone, and I didn't want to disturb him. I am sure he is around here some-where, though. Will this be all for you today?" He asks as he reaches for the magic kit the kids picked out and placed on the counter.

"Yes, this will be all but, I know I saw him up here talking to you just a few minutes ago. He must be waiting outside," she says, shaking her head in confusion.

John rings up their purchase without another word. Abigail could feel his eyes glaring at her during the entire transaction. It was so uncomfortable, and she could not understand why. The town seems so charming, and then there is this weird shop.

*"Maybe it is supposed to be part of the 'experience' of this creepy store, Barbara did say this was a fun place for tourists,"* she ponders to herself as she puts her credit card back into her wallet and grabs the bag turning to leave with her kids.

"Thanks for stopping in, enjoy the rest of your day!" John calls out after them as Abigail and the kids walk toward the exit together.

"Weird, weird man," Abigail whispers.

"Absolutely," Madison agrees.

# CHAPTER 5

*Abigail* glances around the store once more before opening the door, but Lucas is nowhere to be seen inside. They quickly exit hoping to get to Lucas before he gets to upset. She wants this weekend to go well so that they can have a solid chance to reconnect together. Missing how things used to be, before his practice got so big and work took over his entire life. She thought about the years they spent struggling as he built his practice, those were hard years, but some of the best years of her life thus far.

Once outside, they all look around, but Lucas is not among the faces milling about. "Where do you suppose Daddy is?" Abigail asks as she continues to look around her and survey her surroundings. She had sincerely hoped he was waiting for them right outside. She didn't want him to be upset; this getaway was so important to her.

"Maybe he went looking for better cell signal? We all know that is what is most important to him these days anyway," Madison offers with a shrug.

"Well, you would think he could have at least told me where he was going or what he was doing! She replies slightly annoyed while placing her own phone up to her ear calling him. "No answer, ugh!"

After attempting to get a hold of him on his phone with no answer, she resolves to send him a text instead, letting him know that they are going to eat at the diner Barbara mentioned to them earlier and for him to come and meet them there as soon as he got her message.

Abigail walks along in silence, deep in thought, as she leads her kids to the diner. Brody is holding her left hand while Kaitlyn is holding her right one. Madison one step behind. They children chatted cheerfully amongst themselves as they looked into the windows of the shops as they passed by. Once they arrive outside the diner, they are greeted with the most delicious aromas they have ever smelled.

"Now what is that smell?" Kaitlyn asks. "It is making me so hungry! This smells so much better than the magic store did."

"I guess we are about to find out!" Abigail replies as she opens the door to the family style diner.

"Welcome to MawMaw's Country Kitchen! How many are in your party?" A young hostess asks as they walk through the entrance.

"This is absolutely the most adorable restaurant I have ever been to in my entire life!" Abigail gushes, looking around.

Covering each wall is a different type of memorabilia. Filling one from top to bottom was all different types and styles of spoons hanging up for display. The hostess explained that they were something that the founder of the diner had collected over the course of thirty-five years. There were some from all over the world. Patrons often brought her a new one for her collection on their travels, knowing how much she loved and collected them.

Another entire wall featured framed pictures of her ten grandkids—all different ages, starting at birth and continuing throughout their lives. Love and pride were shining through each photo.

"She must be a wonderful woman," Abigail mused as she looked over the pictures while the hostess led them to their booth nearby.

"Oh, there is no one on the planet like MawMaw. Everyone loves her. To know her is to be blessed by the Lord himself!" The hostess gushed.

"How special." Abigail smiled back sweetly while sliding into the booth. "My husband will be meeting us here shortly."

"When he arrives, I will let him know where you are seated. Your server will be with you in just a minute. Enjoy your dinner!"

"Thank you so much."

"Well, this town sure if friendly!" Madison says as the hostess walks back to her stand at the front of the diner. "Perfectly normal, right? Mom, have you ever been to a place that had everyone be so overly friendly?" She continues while cocking her eyebrow to make a point.

"Well, what about that John character? He was absolutely not friendly, he was odd," Abigail argues back, still finding Madison's assessment of the town to be utterly ridiculous.

"That is true, but it does not erase the weirdness of the rest of this town."

Seconds later, a bubbly young server comes bouncing over and greets them cheerfully. After placing their order, the kids settle into playing hangman on the back of their placements while Abigail stares out of the window in the hopes of catching a glimpse of her husband walking by.

"You okay, mom?" Kaitlyn asks, concerned looking up from the game, placing her red crayon down and leaning into the side of Abigail lovingly.

"Yeah, baby, I am fine."

Madison paused and watched her mother carefully without

saying anything before going back to the game with her siblings.

It only took about fifteen minutes before the food was delivered piping hot and looking like it should be pictured for the cover of a magazine. They all ate quietly, enjoying the delicious meal. More than once, Abigail caught herself moaning at the taste of the food as it hit her tongue. Finally, after they have all finished eating every morsel from their plates, and Lucas still hadn't shown up, they get his food boxed to go and decide to head out. Abigail is fighting a war within herself, struggling with her feelings, going back and forth between worry and anger.

"Mom, can we go to the candy shop that Ms. Barbara told us about?" Brody asks with excitement. "I ate all of my food."

Absentmindedly she responds while reaching for her phone inside her purse. "Yeah, sweetie, sure. We can stop by there while we are out looking for daddy."

Abigail quickly dialed Lucas's phone number and again anxiously waited for him to answer. Slamming the phone back into her purse after his voicemail picked up for the third time, she began to feel her anger radiating throughout her entire body. "What in the hell are you doing? This is ridiculous. I don't even know why I bother trying with you anymore!" She mutters under her breath angrily.

"I bet he is just caught up in his work somewhere, Mom; that is all he does anymore anyway. He probably lost track of time. You know how he gets," Madison says, noticing the frustration cross her mother's face.

"I'm sure you're right," Abigail agrees with a slight half-hearted smile.

"You don't think Daddy got eaten by a bear, do you?" questions Brody in fear.

"Oh, Brody, why would you even say such a thing? Gross! No." Madison shouts while shoving her little brother in the arm.

"Ouch! What? That lady said we have to watch for bears!" He cries out in response.

"No, hon, Daddy didn't get eaten by a bear."

*"At least, I sure hope he didn't!"* she thinks to herself in a panic. *"No, we would have heard about that; don't be silly, Abigail,"* she continues to scold herself internally.

"Mom, how do we even know where to look?" Madison asks as they stand outside the country diner looking back and forth down the brick lined streets.

"I don't really know, honey. Let's start by going back to the magic shop. Maybe we will find him around there," Abigail responds as she grabs Brody's hand and leads them back toward the store.

"What about the candy store?" Brody questions panic rising in his voice "You promised we could go to the candy store. You promised!"

"Yes, we can run in there really quick, don't worry." Abigail laughs as they continue walking along. "But you have to be quick, I want to find daddy before it gets dark. We still have to walk back up to the cabin, and I don't want to do that in the dark."

"Okay mom! Brody and Kaitlyn shout with happiness as they skip the rest of the way to the candy shop.

Once they enter Fran's Candy Kitchen, Abigail is not at all surprised to find it decorated as if it was straight out of a time capsule like every other place in this town. It looked exactly like she imagined a candy shop in the fifties looked based on every-thing she had seen in movies and pictures. It was very well maintained and perfectly clean. The store had every kind of candy you could imagine and as the kids looked around with their eyes as big as saucers, they could hardly contain their joy.

"Okay you guys listen up; you can each pick one bag of candy, but you have to be quick remember."

"We will!" Brody shouted as he ran off toward the gummy

worms. Madison and Kaitlyn both went off in their own direction as well and Abigail stood by the window watching for Lucas.

An older woman was standing behind the counter smiling brightly watching the kids as they scurried throughout the store. She looked to be in her seventies and her face just screamed neighborhood grandma. She caught Abigail's eye and nodded cheerfully before Abigail turned back toward the window.

"It's a beautiful day out there isn't it dearie?" She asked from behind her counter.

Abigail turned back to look at the older woman and smiled politely. "Yes, it's nice."

"Your children are adorable," she continued while watching the trio run around trying to decide which candy to pick.

Abigail beamed proudly at the compliment of her children. "Thank you so much, they are pretty great if I do say so myself."

The woman chuckled and went back to wiping down her counter, and Abigail again turned her attention to the sidewalks outside. Searching every single face that came into view hoping for a glimpse of Lucas.

"He isn't out there."

Abigail quickly spun around to find the older woman standing directly behind her with a blank look on her face.

"I'm sorry, what? Are you okay?" Abigail asked surprised and caught off guard by the vacant expression that has replaced the cheerful one that was looking at her just a moment ago.

"You are not going to find him out there," the older woman replies as she turns around and walks slowly back toward the checkout counter.

Abigail stares back at her confused. "What do you mean? How did you know I was looking for my husband? Have you seen him? Do you know where he is?"

Reaching the counter, the older woman ignores the

onslaught of questions coming from Abigail who has followed her, and stares at her impatiently. Suddenly Fran begins speed blinking five times, and then her cheerful disposition is back along with her smile.

"Well?" Abigail asks annoyed.

"Well what dear?"

"What do you know about my husband?" Abigail snaps back at her as the kids walk up holding their bags of candy.

"I am sorry dear I do not know your husband; will this be all for you?" She replies while ringing up the candy the kids have placed on the counter.

"But you just said…. you just told me…. you just said he isn't out there," Abigail stammered in confusion.

"Who isn't out there?"

"My husband!" Abigail answered through gritted teeth.

"Your total is $26.14."

"Answer me damnit!" Abigail yells as she slams her hand on the counter in frustration causing both the older woman and her children to look at her completely baffled by her actions.

"Listen honey, I can see you are upset, and I wish I could help you, but I just sell candy, I don't know a thing about you or your husband!"

Madison looks between the older woman and her mother embarrassed. "What is wrong with you?"

Abigail glances at Madison before turning back to Fran and shaking her head. "I apologize, I thought I heard you say something else I guess."

Madison rolls her eyes and grabs the bag of candies off the counter before reaching for Brody's hand and leading him toward the door. Abigail looks at the stunned shop owner and nods her head in apology once again before taking Kaitlyn's hand and following behind Madison and Brody.

"What in the world was that?" Madison shouts once they get outside. "How incredibly embarrassing, are you losing your freaking marbles? You just yelled at an old woman about dad like she should know where he is!" She continued while flailing her arms about. "Don't take your marriage problems out on strangers selling candy! Good grief. I am so glad we won't have to see these people again, if you did this at home I would have to move!"

"Oh, stop it Madison, it wasn't that big of a deal, and I apologized. I just heard her wrong."

Madison rolled her eyes and turned her back to her mother in disgust. "Whatever mom."

Feeling slightly embarrassed at her behavior and worry beginning to creep in over where Lucas could be Abigail leads to kids back toward the magic shop to hopefully find Lucas.

*"If I am being honest, that woman was slightly creepy, I mean she had such a blank expression, like she was a zombie. Oh Abigail, get it together, maybe I am losing my marbles,"* she thought to herself as she walked along the sidewalk with the kids.

"I want to go back to the cabin. I was really looking forward to using the hot tub!" Kaitlyn whines.

"Me too, honey. Me too! Hopefully, we will find him soon! We can't go back until we find him, though," Abigail responds while patting her on her back in consolation.

"Maybe Daddy went back to the cabin," Brody offers.

"Maybe. That would explain him not answering his phone since the service is not very good up there. But I can't imagine why he would go back there without telling us," Abigail slowly answers, pondering the idea. "That wouldn't make sense."

"He probably wasn't even thinking," Madison states with an attitude and a shrug.

"Let's just run back to the magic shop and double-check really quick first," Abigail decides as they continue off in that direction.

As they walk along the sidewalk, Abigail sees someone waving at them. She recognizes the woman as Barbara from earlier and realizes that she is standing there talking with a police officer, so she quickly jogs over to where they are talking.

"Excuse me, officer. I am sorry to interrupt, but I was wondering if I could get your help."

"Of course, ma'am. What can I do for you?" the officer responds, turning towards her giving her his full attention.

"I can't find my husband. It has been a few hours now; he isn't answering his phone and I have no idea where he is!" She explains with panic showing in her voice.

"Oh no, darlin'. Let me know if I can do anything for you. I'll catch up with you later, Jason," Barbara offers with a smile of sympathy to Abigail and heads off down the street.

The officer, Jason, early thirties, with a head shaved nearly bald and muscles bulging inside his uniform, pulls out a small notebook from his shirt pocket and begins asking Abigail questions while taking notes.

"What is your name, your husband's name, when and where was the last time, you saw him?"

"My name is Abigail Ferguson, and my husband is Lucas Ferguson. We just arrived here in town today for an extended weekend vacation. We were all together when we walked down here into town earlier this afternoon. We met Barbara, and she told us about a few places we should visit. Next, we went to the Mystical Magical Emporium right over there. Lucas was on his phone working on the other side of the store from where the kids and I were shopping. When we were ready to check out, I couldn't find him in the store anywhere. I tried to call him, but he didn't answer. We just assumed he had wandered off to take a phone call or something. He was worried about his work when we arrived and was having difficulty getting service on his phone. Since he wasn't answering and we were getting hungry, I texted him where we were going and to meet us there when he was done with whatever he was doing. He never showed up, and he still isn't answering any of my texts or calls!"

Cocking an eyebrow, he looks skeptically at Abigail "Wait, let me get this straight, you couldn't find your husband, and you went out to eat instead of looking for him?"

"Well, to be fair, I didn't think it was a problem at first. I just assumed he was off on his phone somewhere, like always. He has been very busy with work and just took on a stressful new case. In all honesty, I was a little annoyed that he went off without us and without even telling me where he was going," she snaps back defensively.

"Okay, so, he goes off on his own a lot then?"

"No, not necessarily. I meant he is working on his phone a lot. But his phone wasn't getting a very good signal anywhere, and he was really stressed out about the case he is working on. He is a criminal defense attorney, and like I said, he just took on a new case that has been consuming all of his time," she attempts to explain.

"Have you tried to locate his phone?"

"No, I don't have a tracking app on his phone; I just have them on the phones for the kids."

"Now, please do not take offense to the next question, but were you folks having any trouble at home?"

"What? No! Well, not any more than the next marriage anyway. Seriously, can you help me find him or not?" Abigail demands, getting frustrated with the line of question.

"It hasn't been that long since the last time you have seen him. Technically as a rule we don't get involved this early in cases like this, as the missing person usually turns up on their own after a few hours. However, I can see how worried you are, and I am not currently busy so I am going to go ahead and see what I can do to help you find your husband. I promise you, ma'am, I will do my best to locate him for you. Where is your family staying while you are here visiting?"

"We are renting the Bibler cabin up the ridge," Abigail responds, pointing toward the mountains behind her.

"Okay, why don't you and the kids head on up to the cabin and see if he happened to go back up there. Show me a picture of him, and I will have a look around town. I will swing by the cabin with any news. It is going to be getting dark soon, and you don't want to be running around in the dark with the kids," he offers politely.

"Okay, we were going to stop over at the magic shop one more time and double-check in case he is waiting for us over there, then we will go back and see if he for some strange reason went back to the cabin without us."

Abigail pulls out her phone and shows the officer pictures of Lucas.

"Again, his name is Lucas; he is about 5'11, 195lbs, and has a muscular build. He is very busy and always working on his phone. So, the fact that he hasn't answered any of my calls or texts in the last few hours, or at least found us, is very upsetting. I am getting really worried that something is terribly wrong!"

"Okay, I will have a look around, see what I can find out. My best guess is you will find him back at your cabin," Jason states assuredly, closing his notebook and putting it back in his shirt pocket.

"I really hope so, but I have a hard time believing he would just up and leave us alone in a strange town, just to go back to the cabin. Especially knowing there is a chance that there will be no signal for his phone up there. That just does not make any sense," she replies, unsure.

Abigail thanks Jason for his help and walks off down the sidewalk with the kids. Once they reach the magic store, Abigail looks around outside before grabbing the door handle to step inside. A sense of dread washes over her as she opens the door. Then, with the kids all tagging closely behind, she makes her way over to John, who is sitting behind the register fiddling with that weird hat.

"Welcome back," he greets ominously.

"Hi there, I was wondering, have you by any chance seen my husband come back by here? We have not seen him since we left your store, and I am starting to get very worried," she asks while scanning the aisles of the store.

"No, ma'am. I am sorry, but I haven't seen him," he replies, shaking his head with an odd smirk.

"That is so strange. Where could he be? If you do happen to see him, would you please let him know that we are going back to our cabin and he can find us up there?" she asks, visibly concerned.

"I sure will," he nods back and returns to work on the strange hat in his hands.

"Why don't you throw that gross thing away?" Kaitlyn asks, scrunching up her nose.

"Never, it holds a special place in my heart."

"I think it's yucky," she continues.

"Kaitlyn, now that isn't nice. Apologize so we can go," Abigail scolds.

"Sorry, I was just saying. But if you like it," she replies softly with a shrug.

"Okay, kiddos, I guess we will go back and check and see if he went to our rental. Seems strange he would go back without us, but stranger things have happened, I suppose," Abigail says as she leads her children back out of the store.

As Abigail and the kids begin their trek through the woods back to their weekend rental cabin, the children seem somewhat relaxed and enjoy playful banter amongst themselves. "I can't believe that Lucas has obviously been so absent that he goes missing for several hours and the kids think nothing of it," Abigail murmurs to herself as she listens to her kids while they walk.

"I am glad we are going back before it gets dark. This way, we can watch out for bears!" Brody exclaims with relief.

"Oh, Brody, you and your bears," Madison replies while playfully punching her brother in the shoulder. "Even if we did see a bear, it wouldn't want to eat you! You are so tiny you wouldn't even be a good snack!"

"Well, that is reassuring," he laughs back.

"My legs are tired, I don't want to walk anymore," Kaitlyn whines.

"Kaitlyn, all of our legs hurt, how else do you plan on getting back to the cabin? You aren't a baby, no one is going to carry you," Madison snaps back.

"Sweetie, the cabin is super close, just hold on and keep walking we will be there soon, okay?" Abigail asks softly.

Kaitlyn nods her head and the group continue to walk without issue for a few more minutes when the cabin comes into view. They all take off running toward it getting a second wind in the hopes of finding Lucas inside. As they all rush in the front door, out of breath from running, everyone starts calling out for the family's patriarch.

"Daddy?" Brody hollers while jogging from room to room.

"Dad? *Dad*? Where are you?" Madison yells, rushing past Brody to check the back deck.

"Daddy?" Kaitlyn says as she begins to cry uncontrollably.

Loudly as she runs throughout the cabin, Abigail yells, "Lucas, are you here?"

"Mom, Daddy isn't here!" Madison says, worry beginning to form on her teenage face.

"Mommy, where is he? I am scared," Kaitlyn says, continuing to cry.

"I know, honey. Mommy is too, but we will find him," Abigail says, reassuring her kids while trying to push the panic out of her chest.

"Mom let's just drive back into town in the car and look for him," Madison says, grabbing ahold of Brody's hand and walking toward the front door in determination.

"Definitely, let me write him a note really quick in case we miss him in passing."

Abigail scribbles a note quickly onto a piece of paper and leaves it on the kitchen table:

*Lucas, the kids, and I have been looking for you everywhere. We are going back into town to look for you again. If you are reading this, call me if your phone is working. If not, stay here until we get back! I love you.*

# CHAPTER 6

*A*s Abigail drives down the dark roads and dimly lit streets of the town the kids look out of the windows, searching and calling for their father. Finally, after almost an hour, Abigail sees Jason, the officer from earlier, pulling up behind her and motioning for her to stop.

"Maybe he found Daddy!" Abigail exclaims with hope as she quickly pulls over to the side of the road. Parking underneath a flickering streetlight she watches him from the side mirror as he walks toward her, he has a look of concern on his face. "That doesn't look like the face of someone who is coming to tell me he found Lucas," she whispers to herself.

"Howdy, ma'am. I assume since you are out here yelling your husband's name out of your windows, he wasn't there at your cabin like we had hoped," he questions as he leans onto the side of her car peering inside at the kids in the backseat before turning his attention back to Abigail.

"No, he wasn't there. So, I left a note for him, letting him know we were going to drive back down here and look for him again. The kids and I are franticly worried at this point. There is no reason why we shouldn't have found him by now."

"Mrs. Ferguson, listen, I sympathize with your fear. However, after I left from speaking with you, I did go around and talk to all the local shop owners. Unfortunately, no one has seen him. There is no trace of him anywhere. I am going to go back to John's shop and look around, and I'll question him again first thing in the morning. However, aside from that, I have nothing to go on here. Now, I feel like I need to be honest with you. It looks to me like he may have run off. It could be one of those situations where he just needed some time alone to clear his head and after he has done that, he will come back remorseful for what he put you through while he was away."

"*What*? What are you saying?" Abigail exclaims, shocked and angry.

"Look, I am not trying to be so blunt, but in my opinion and in my experience, these types of cases are usually domestic, and the spouse turns up after a cooling off period. Sometimes with the dreaded papers and sometimes with an apology," he offers with a shrug.

"My husband did not just leave us! He would never do that, not to me or to the kids! Especially the kids! If you are not going to take this seriously and help me find him, then I am wasting my time even talking to you," she snarls through gritted teeth and drives away, leaving the officer staring after her.

Looking into the rear-view mirror at her children sadness overtakes her and she feels her body begin to tremble. Kaitlyn and Brody are crying softly, and Madison looked worried for the first time since Lucas went missing.

"What are we going to do Mom?" Madison asked quietly.

"We are going to find your father, that is what we are going to do," Abigail replied as she choked down a sob.

"That cop said dad ran away, you don't think that is true, do you?" Madison questions just above a whisper, almost so silently that Abigail barely heard her.

"No, absolutely not. He would never, don't think that way for one more second."

Madison lets out a deep sigh and puts her earbuds into her ears slouching down in her seat. Abigail watched her carefully as she continued to look through the window in search for her husband and fight the tears threatening to spill down her cheeks.

Grabbing ahold of her phone, Abigail frantically dials while struggling to breathe as all her fears start rushing to the surface at once.

"Hello?" she hears from the other end of the line.

"Allison, I need you," was all Abigail could say before she started sobbing into the phone.

# CHAPTER 7

"Honey, what is it? What's wrong?"

"It's Lucas, he is missing," she manages to choke out before totally breaking down.

"What? What do you mean missing? What are you talking about?" Panic rising in her best friend's voice.

"I, I don't know. He is just missing. I don't know what to do."

"Abigail, listen to me. Send me the address to the cabin you are staying at. Give me a few minutes to throw some things in a bag, Benjamin and I will get on the road within the next fifteen minutes," Allison replies as she runs to her room and starts grabbing things out of her dresser and tossing them onto her bed.

Benjamin chases after her, worried, seeing the look on her face and watching her run around their room throwing things all over their bed.

"What is going on?" He whispers in a panic. "Who are you talking to?"

Allison just shakes her head at him and continues to toss things frantically as she fights back her own tears.

"Thank you, Allison. I really need you. I am sorry to make

you do this, but I don't think I can hold it together much longer."

"Do not thank me; that's what best friends are for. Let me finish getting ready and I will call you from the road. Don't forget to text me the address."

"Ben, Lucas is missing!" Allison yells as she hangs up the phone and begins shoving things in a teal oversized tote bag. "We have to go! We have to go right now."

"What the hell do you mean Lucas is missing?" Benjamin asks, staring back at his wife dumbfounded.

"I don't know, but we have to go! We can discuss it from the truck, I don't have a lot of details. Get some clothes quick, she is going to text us the address. They are only a few hours from here."

Less than fifteen minutes later they are running out the front door slamming it behind them as they rush toward their vehicle in the driveway.

"This cannot be happening!" Benjamin comments as Allison tosses their bag into the truck and hops in quickly. He guns the engine and looks over at his wife who has tears streaming down her face, he grabs her hand and squeezes gently. "It's going to be ok Allie."

She nods back in silence.

They drive along in quietude for a few hours, neither sure of what to say, both worried about what they will find when they get to Cranston Creek, and how they will handle whatever it is.

"I am going to call Abigail and let her know we will be there soon, find out where to meet her," Allison mutters, half to herself and half to Benjamin. She dials the phone and puts it on speaker so he can hear her too. It starts to ring.

"Allison, where are you?"

"We are almost there honey, we are coming as fast as we can. Any news? Where should we meet you?"

"No, nothing. I am on my way back to the rental. It is so late. The kids are sleeping in the backseat. Meet me back there."

"Okay, we will be there within the next twenty minutes. Just hold on."

Abigail lets out a deep sigh and hangs up the phone. *"I can't believe they both dropped everything and came down here to help me."* Freely letting her tears fall while looking at her children sleeping in the back seat, she pulls into the driveway of their vacation home. Taking a deep breath and wiping her cheeks with the back of her hands she walks around to the back of the car and gently nudges Madison awake.

"Come on, Madison. Wake up, sweetie. I need you to walk into the cabin for me," she whispers.

"Did we find Dad?" Madison asks, eyes still half-closed from exhaustion.

"No honey, not yet," Abigail replies sadly.

"Then what are we doing?" Madison questions, frantically jumping up in her seat, suddenly wide awake.

"Honey, it is two o'clock in the morning. I need you guys to get into bed. We will start looking again first thing in the morning," Abigail assures her daughter. "Benjamin and Allison will be in any minute. They are going to help."

"But Dad!"

"I know honey, but I have to take care of you guys too, please don't fight me on this, I am too exhausted to argue."

Madison nods back at her mother and climbs slowly out of the car as Abigail wakes up Kaitlyn and lifts a sleeping Brody into her arms and begins to carry him toward the cabin. Madison and Kaitlyn groggily follow behind.

After tucking the kids in and making sure they are back to sleep, Abigail sits on the edge of Brody's bed and stares at each of them with tears in her eyes. Kaitlyn stirs awake and looks at her mother with sadness.

"Mommy is Daddy dead?" she asks quietly.

"No. No, honey. We can't think like that. We will find Daddy!" She says hoping to reassure her daughter even though she was unsure herself.

"Well, then where could he be?" Kaitlyn questions doubtfully. "Where is he sleeping tonight?"

"I don't know, honey; I just don't know. We are going to have to pray that we find him in the morning."

Madison, who is sharing a bed with Kaitlyn, begins to awaken to the sounds of chatter. Sitting up in her bed, she rubs her eyes and runs her hands through her hair, thinking about what she wants to ask before speaking.

"Mom, I know I already asked you this but, do you think the police officer was right? Do you think Daddy could have just left us?"

Abigail looks off into space and contemplates for a minute before answering her daughter. All she had was questions, and no answers. "No, I don't think that's possible, I don't think that Daddy would ever do that. You three were everything to him; he would never just up and leave you. Never. I know that without a shadow of a doubt.

Brody woke up during the conversation and was laying back watching Abigail and listening intently. He slowly got up and crawled down to the end of the bed where Abigail was sitting and curled up into her lap.

"Then why didn't he act like it, Mommy? Every time I asked Daddy to play with me, he would say five more minutes and then would just ignore me," Brody whines sadly. "I tried to show him my match box car collection and he didn't even look."

Abigail begins to rub Brody's back softly in consolation. Looking over at her daughters the same distraught look on both of their faces she had no idea what to say in order to make them feel better in this moment. Do they not feel loved? Has she failed as a mother? Was she providing enough love? Is she meeting their needs?

"I am so sorry, baby. I need you to trust me on this, though, daddy does love you. He loves each one of you so much. I know he has been so super busy with his work lately, which in turn as made him not act like himself lately. However, that does not change for one second the fact that he loves you all. Please know how much we both love you."

"I have never heard of someone working so much that they didn't want their family anymore," Madison states flatly.

"Daddy doesn't want us anymore?" Kaitlyn gasps as tears begin to well up in her eyes.

"Okay, calm down! Of course, daddy still wants us. You cannot listen to that officer; he doesn't even know daddy! Try to get some sleep; we are going to get up early in the morning to go back out there and look for him."

Softly Madison questions her mother as she lays back down and pulls the blanket up to her chin, "What if we don't find him though, Mom?"

Abigail ignores the question and gets up to leave the room. As she opens the bedroom door to exit, she hears tires crunching on the gravel drive out front and realizes with great relief that her friends have arrived to help her figure this whole nightmare out.

"You guys get some sleep; I love you all very much!" She says as she turns off the light and closes the door to the bedroom, leaving the children to hopefully get some rest.

Opening the front door, Abigail is almost knocked over as Allison embraces her so quickly. Crying onto each other's shoulders, Benjamin pushes past the two friends and brings in their bags.

"You guys can have that room over there," Abigail says to Benjamin as she points to a bedroom across from them. Then, grabbing hold of Allison, she leads her to the couch.

Benjamin tosses their bags onto the bed and joins the women in the living room. Taking a seat on the recliner across from the women, he places his elbows on his knees and leans in to offer his support.

"Abigail, what happened?" Allison asks quietly while rubbing her hand along her friend's arm soothingly.

"I honestly have no idea." Abigail recounts their day and fills them in on everything that has happened since the family arrived in Cranston Creek earlier that day. They all sit there, speechless and unsure of what could have happened. All three stay together in the living room, talking and trying to plan their next steps. After a few hours, they have all fallen asleep where they were sitting. Abigail and Allison are sleeping cuddled together on the couch, both with puffy eyes from crying themselves to sleep.

Early the next day, Abigail is startled awake by the sound of a loud knock on the front door. Benjamin and Allison both sit up straight and watch as Abigail runs to the front door while whispering, "please be Lucas."

Abigail quickly unlocks the door and flings it open. However, to her sheer disappointment, the knock did not come from Lucas, but from officer Jason, along with another officer who has joined him. Looking disheartened, she opens the door further while slowly stepping aside to let them in.

Allison and Benjamin stand up from where their respective seats and make their way over to Abigail, wrapping their arms around her in support of whatever the officers are going to say.

"Officers, did you find my husband?" She questions with both anticipation and fear.

"No, ma'am, unfortunately we haven't found him yet. However, I did want to apologize for last night; I was out of line, and I am sorry. I also wanted to let you know that we have a put together a search party, and they are out there right now looking for him."

"Thank you!" Abigail exclaims, letting out a sigh of relief.

"If you don't mind me asking, who are these people?" Jason asks, motioning to Benjamin and Allison.

"Sure, they're our best friends and also our neighbors back home. I called Allison last night, letting her know what was going on, and she and her husband Benjamin drove down right away."

"I see." Jason offers while looking between the trio suspiciously.

"You see what?" Abigail snaps, still annoyed with Jason from the night before.

"I am sure he didn't mean anything by it, right officer?" Benjamin says coolly.

"No, of course not. I am sorry if it came across as an accusation. Just so you know after we leave here, we are going to head back over to John's place to see if we can find anything over there in the daylight. I will keep you posted," he responds somberly.

"Something is off with that man and his store. I mean, I realize that you obviously know him better than I do, being as I have only been here for one day. However, I am one hundred percent sure that I saw Lucas talking to that store owner. When I asked him about it, he acted like they he hadn't even spoken to Lucas at all. And don't get me started on his creepy facial expressions. It doesn't make any sense."

"Well, we are going to go ahead and go over there now. I will let you know what we find out as soon as we get any information," Officer Jason says as he and his partner walk out of the cabin and head toward their cruiser.

Abigail closes the door slowly, feeling the weight of her stress and worry crashing down onto her. She leans up against the back of the door and slides down to the floor, placing her head into her hands, and weeps. From the floor, she begins to pray silently. *"Lord, please let the search party find Lucas. Please, let him be okay and come back to us. Please do not make me go on without him."*

Benjamin and Allison sit down on the floor next to her and let her cry. They each have a hand resting softly on her back in comfort.

"I'm sorry you guys, I can't seem to get my emotions under control. I am so scared," she sobs into her hands.

"Sweetie, it's totally understandable, anyone in your situation would be the same way. If you want to cry these two shoulders right here will be ready and waiting for you at any time," Allison says with compassion as she points to each of her shoulders and leans toward Abigail wrapping her arms around her.

"Mommy?" Brody calls from the bedroom.

Abigail wipes her face with her hands and takes a deep calming breath. Allison nods to her friend in support as they all stand to their feet. Allison and Benjamin go back and sit on the couch while Abigail walks quickly into the bedroom where her children were sleeping. She curls up next to Brody and holds him close for a minute in silence.

"Are we ever going to find Daddy?" he asks sadly.

"Yes, baby. We are going to find Daddy," she responds, running her fingers through his hair. "Let's all get ready and go back into town to start looking again, okay?"

"Are Allison and Benjamin here?" Madison asks sitting up and shaking Kaitlyn awake beside her.

"Yeah, they are in the living room waiting for us, so take turns getting dressed in the bathroom and come out to the living room when you are ready, and we will get going.

Everyone got ready as quickly as they could, no one caring much about their appearance and they loaded up and headed back into town in the hopes of finding Lucas today, before it is too late.

# CHAPTER 8

*L*ucas opens his eyes and finds himself lying on the floor in an unfamiliar room, confused and alone. His body aches and his head is spinning. Laying still looking up at the ceiling for a moment he attempts to gather his thoughts. Then, finally, he begins to sit up, puzzled and shaken he slowly looks around the room to survey his surroundings. Black walls, a dimly lit lamp sitting on a small side table next to a single twin-sized bed, a small table, and a lone wooden chair.

*What is going on? Where am I? How did I get here?*

As he continues to survey the room, he realizes that there is no door. Panic sets in, and he begins to bang on the walls screaming for help.

"Hello! Hello! Abigail? Kids? Anyone? Somebody help me!"

Suddenly, he notices something out of the corner of his eye, John is now sitting at the small table with his hands folded in front of him. A small smirk planted on his face.

"Lucas," John begins.

"Man, what is going on? How did you get in here? How do I get out of here?" Lucas asks angrily.

"Lucas, I think it is time for a little self-reflection," John continues calmly.

"What are you talking about? Self-reflection? Let me out of here!"

Lucas lunges for the older man, but John dodges out of the way at the last second, and Lucas falls to the floor with a loud thud next to the chair that has toppled over after John leapt out of it so quickly.

"Now, we are not going to have any of that," John states gruffly. "You are safe. Your family is safe. However, you, are going to remain in this room for a while," he explains.

"Why? If it's money you want, I will get you money. Whatever it is you want, it's yours. I don't know why you are doing this, but I promise you, I won't turn you in or say anything to anyone. Just let me go back to my wife and kids. I can assure you that we will never come back here again!" Lucas pleads.

"I am sorry, but I cannot let you leave yet. I will be back later with some food. In the meantime, I suggest you think about your life, your family, career, all of it. Also, while you are in this room you can use this iPad. It will allow you to see and hear your family. They can't see you, but you can see them at all times," John states as he slides a tablet over to Lucas. Looking down at the device, Lucas watches as his wife and children worry over where he is.

"Is this live?" Lucas asks.

"Yes."

"How? How does this work? Are they being followed?"

"Lucas, you came into my *magic* shop, did you seriously think that I couldn't do magic?"

"But magic isn't real, it's just an illusion."

John stared at Lucas, cocking his eyebrow and smirking.

"They are freaking out! Why won't you let me go to them? Just tell me what you want! I will do anything you ask," Lucas yells in frustration

"I don't want anything from you."

John walks over to the farthest wall and begins to lean up against it.

Realization washes over Lucas as he watches John's silhouette in the dimly lit room, running his hand along the wall slowly. The movements were almost unrecognizable.

"I can't let you out of here, Lucas, not yet anyway. I can assure you that you will understand soon enough though."

"What? What does that even mean?" Lucas questioned while looking back down at the tablet. Abigail was sitting at a restaurant with the kids. She pulled out her phone to call him. Instinctively he reaches for his pocket, but his phone is not there.

"Oh, are you looking for this?" John asks while shaking the phone from side to side.

"Yes!"

"I have to be honest; I am surprised it took you ten minutes to start looking for it," John says mockingly as he lifts the phone above his head and slams it to the ground before stomping on it with his right heel.

"NOOOO! Why would you do that? I need that for work!" Lucas screamed as he dove onto the floor toward the phone.

"Pathetic," John murmurs kicking the remains of the phone toward the middle of the room watching as Lucas scrambled after it, scooping the shattered phone into his hands and placing it onto the table. Movement on the tablet causes Lucas to look back over at it and watch his family exit the diner and begin looking all around obviously searching for him.

"Look at my wife! She is so worried! Why are you doing this?" Lucas asks, holding up the tablet to John angrily.

"I am not the one doing this Lucas, you are."

Frustrated, he drops the tablet back in front of him and continues to watch his family. The next time he looks up, John is gone. Quickly he makes his way over to the wall where John had just been standing. Running his fingers carefully over the area that he thought he saw John touching earlier, he felt for something, anything that would get him out of this room. Then he found it, a small area just slightly squishier than the rest of the area. Lucas put his ear against the wall and could hear nothing. Then, realizing what he had done, he silently berates himself.

*What am I doing? Of course, I can't hear anything; this is a wall. Being stupid is not going to get me out of here!*

"Now or never," he states to himself as he jams his finger into the softer area, and in an instant, he is standing inside the back of the magic shop. "What the hell? How did that happen?"

With no time to think, he takes off running toward the front door as fast as he can. Desperate to find his family and get out of town, he ignores the pain shooting through his head and continues to run. As he sprints toward the exit, he hears John coming up behind him.

"*Stop!*"

Lucas kept running, flinging the door open as soon as he reached it and dashes out quickly. However, when he gets outside, everything seems off somehow. It was eerily quiet, completely opposite of when they were out there earlier. There was no one around, no sound of children laughing or playing, no families chatting or enjoying the outdoors. The shops all looked dark, dingy even, but the sun was just beginning to set. An ominous fog seemed to have settled in over the entire town.

Not wanting John to catch up to him, Lucas continued running down the street toward the diner that he saw Abigail and the kids at on the iPad.

"Where do you think you are going?" John yells after him.

Lucas did not even bother to turn around; he reached the diner in record time and was shocked to find the door locked. He tugged on it a couple times then gave it one more yank as hard as he could. When it did not open, he began shaking it, followed by loudly banging, screaming for someone to open the door. When nothing happened, and he heard no sounds coming from inside, he walked over to the window. Peering in confirmed that it was closed and looked as if it had been closed for years.

"How can that be? They were just here not that long ago," he commented to himself under his breath, looking around frantically.

He catches a glimpse of John slowly strolling towards him like he had not a care in the world, and knows he needs to act fast to get away from the kidnapper. Looking back and forth down the deserted street Lucas noticed a single car parked a few stores down. Making a beeline for it, he heard John calling out behind him.

"You ARE going to come back with me, Lucas! Might as well make it easy on yourself and come with me now."

Ignoring John, Lucas continued to his destination as quickly as he could, hoping he would be able to do what he was planning on doing after he got inside the car. Then, breathing heavily, he yanked the door open and frantically hopped in.

"It's like riding a bike, if only my colleagues could see me now," Lucas whispers as he hotwires the car quickly, jerking the stolen car into gear and mashing onto the gas with a look of determination on his face. Speeding past John as he heads toward the cabin.

"You can't run away from me, Lucas."

"Watch me!" he shouts back as the car lurches forward, tires squealing as he drives away from his abductor.

Since the town was oddly abandoned, Lucas decided Abigail must have taken the kids back to the cabin, and he headed that way. He has every intention of grabbing his family and getting out of this town asap. However, as he flies up the driveway of the rental house, the gravel flying in the air behind him, he is disappointed to find that the family car is not there. Jumping out of the car and quickly running through the front door, his heart sank into his stomach at what he did not find inside.

"Abigail! Where are you?"

# CHAPTER 9

*A*bigail, Allison, Benjamin, and the kids are sitting at a picnic table near the woods, eating sandwiches in silence. They had been searching for Lucas for several hours to no avail. As they look around them, they realize that there had to be at least 50 strangers in bright orange vests also searching for the family man. Brody breaks the silence as he starts to cry.

"We are never going to see Daddy again, are we?"

"Honey, we can't give up; we can't think like that! Daddy needs us to be strong for him. We are not giving up," Abigail responds lovingly.

"Mom let's be real. It has been almost another entire day. Look at all the people that are helping to look for him. Where could he be? That officer was right. Dad left us!" Madison states flatly, dropping her sandwich on the table in angst.

"Madison, do you really think Daddy left us?" Kaitlyn cries sadly.

"Kids please, just stop. This is not helping," Abigail scolds. She notices Officer Jason walking over toward their table and motioning for Abigail to come to speak with him. She looks at

Allison, who gives her a nod. Once she makes her way over, she stares at him somberly, waiting to hear what he has to say.

"Mrs. Ferguson, I need to speak with you for a minute. As you know, we went back to the magic shop and spoke with John. We found absolutely nothing to suggest he was ever even in Cranston Creek. If it wasn't for John confirming that he did in fact see Lucas with you I would have a hard time believing he was ever here.

"I'm confused, what are you saying?"

"There was no sign of your husband at the Mystical Magical Emporium, there was no sign of him anywhere," he states flatly.

"Well, a person can't just vanish; he has to be around here somewhere!" She yells with terror in her voice. "We came here for a mini-vacation, time to get away and enjoy some quality family time together without work! How can this be happening?"

Officer Jason looks at her with a flash of compassion in his eyes and drops his head a little.

"Maybe that is what this weekend meant to you. But are you sure that is what it meant to Mr. Ferguson?" he asks slowly.

"The idea that my husband just up and left us while on vacation, in another state, where we don't know a single person is just the most asinine thing I have ever heard. He wouldn't do that; how would he have even left anyway? I have our car!" she shouts in anger, arms flailing wildly.

"Mrs. Ferguson, I need you to listen to me for a minute. Cranston Creek is a very small and extremely safe town. The most excitement we get around here is when a tourist leaves food out and a bear gets into it. We have virtually zero crime, and in your husbands' case, we have no crime scene. There is absolutely nothing to go on here."

"What exactly are you saying?" Abigail demands, beginning to panic. "Lucas is somewhere!"

"Well, we are going to continue our investigation; the search party is going to continue to look for Lucas. However, my recommendation for you and your children is to go on back home. Try to keep them in a routine for stability. We will keep you up to date on what we have going on here. If by some chance he shows up back at home, then you can let us know that too," he offers solemnly.

"Officer, I'm sorry, are you serious? I mean, are you one hundred percent seriously serious right now? Do you have any idea how incredibly stupid you sound? You want me to just go home? Go back home without my husband? How am I supposed to do that? What am I supposed to tell my kids?" she asks, dumbfounded at even the idea of leaving without Lucas.

"I would tell them the truth, you are going home, and there is a search party and a lot of trained individuals that are going to continue looking for their Daddy," he offers.

"I am not going to go home without my husband, and I can tell you right now that they are not going to want to make the drive back home without their father either! We can stay here and help with the search!" She argues back in frustration. "I can promise you this, I am not going to be leaving this town until we find Lucas!"

"Mrs. Ferguson, there is not a single person in this entire town that has seen him since you reported him missing. There are no footprints to follow, no leads to track down. We are looking for a ghost!" He insists. "I am telling you that this is not a situation for your kids to be in. Trust me, as soon as we have any information, no matter how insignificant, we will get a hold of you!" he reassures her.

"I absolutely expect you to get a hold of me; however, I am *not* leaving. You can stop with that nonsense because it is not happening. Don't even bother mentioning it to me again, it is only making me angry and wasting precious time that could be being spent finding Lucas!"

"Mrs. Ferguson, look at your children. They are crying; you have to get them out of here," he replies softly with compassion.

Abigail glances over at her kids. Abigail has her arm wrapped around Kaitlyn and Brody is talking with Benjamin while Madison has her head laying on her arms perched on the tabletop. They all look heartbroken and miserable. She contemplates everything the officer has said and knows that leaving is not going to fix the broken hearts of any of them.

"So, let me get this straight, if your wife was missing and you were on vacation, you would just go home without her? Do you even hear how freaking ridiculous that sounds?" she asks accusingly.

"Of course not, but I am a police officer. I am highly trained in these types of situations."

"Great, then use your training and find my husband, but I am not leaving until you do!"

Jason reaches for her shoulder to calm her down, but Abigail, who is already over the top angry at the entire conversation, shakes him off and storms back to her children and friends who have been watching the interaction and are anxious to hear what is going on.

"You okay, mommy?" Kaitlyn asks, concerned. "Why were you arguing with the police officer?"

"We just had a difference of opinion, that's all. It is fine," she mutters before tears began to stream down her cheeks.

"Mommy?" Kaitlyn questions siding up next to her mother and wrapping her arms around her waist while beginning to cry into her side.

"What did he say?" Allison asks, rubbing her friends back gently.

"Nothing of any use. He thinks that I should just go home! Can you imagine?" She shouts angrily while continuing to cry.

"What? No one in their right mind would do that. Why

would he even suggest something so stupid?" Benjamin asks, turning to watch Jason walk away.

"That is exactly what I said," Abigail replies as she hiccups. "I will not be leaving here until Lucas is in the car coming home with us!"

"Of course not honey, I wouldn't either. We are going to find him, kids, do you hear me? We are going to find your daddy and we will all go home together, okay?"

"I sure hope so, but where do you suppose he was all night then?" Madison questions.

"That is just one more thing we are going to have to figure out, but we will, together."

"Yes, now let's finish up eating and get back to looking," Benjamin offers with a fake smile directed toward the kids, hoping that it looked genuine enough to calm their fears, wishing he could believe what they were all saying himself. However, his rational brain had so many of his own questions. Where was Lucas all night? What could he possibly be doing? Where in the world could he be? The only conclusion he could come up with at the moment was that this situation does not look good at all.

# CHAPTER 10

*A*fter running through and searching the entire cabin and finding no sign of his wife or kids, Lucas goes into the kitchen to grab a knife from the butcher block in case he is trapped by John again. Pacing the living room behind the sofa, he stops abruptly when he realizes something. Jogging over to the bedroom he was supposed to be sharing with Abigail, he flings open the door and looks around carefully, panic beginning to set it. He slings the closet door open, only to find it empty and dusty. Dropping to his knees, he scans underneath the bed and the dresser drawers and sees nothing but empty space. He rushes to the bedroom next door that the kids would be staying in and does the same thing. None of their stuff is in there either. He takes a minute to gather his thoughts and sits on the couch in the living room. Running his hand along the fabric, he realizes that while this couch looks like the couch that was here when they arrived, it couldn't possibly be the same one. It was faded and worn, where the couch earlier looked brand new.

"I must be in the wrong cabin!" He realizes with relief as he runs onto the porch ready to head to the correct place and find his family. However, a large wooden sign that says *'Bibler Cabin'* is hanging above the front door. "Okay, I am in the right place, so where is our stuff? Why is everything different? Where is everyone from the town? Maybe I have been drugged because nothing else is making any sense. I bet John put something in that sandwich. Okay, I just need a minute to think things through."

Lucas begins to get antsy. Where could Abigail possibly be? Should he go back into town and risk being found by John? Should he just sit and wait for her? After carefully pondering his options, he concluded that he should stay; she would recognize that everything was closed and return. Sitting on the bench outside the cabin on the wrap-around porch, he waits for the sound of a car. Turning his head to look inside the window, he carefully examines the cabin's interior. Why is everything inside so incredibly different than what I remember? This does not make any sense. He goes back and forth between pacing the porch and sitting on the bench, but after waiting for a couple of hours, the worry overtakes him; he goes back out to the stolen car and attempts to get it to start. He is going to find his family and get them out of here. However, he still cannot get the engine to turnover after several attempts. Finally, he looks at the gauges when he realizes that the car is out of gas. Slamming his hand on the steering wheel, he sets off jogging back where he came from.

"I cannot believe this is happening! What are the odds? Can this vacation get any worse? Please Lord don't let this get any worse. I have got to find Abigail and the kids and get us out of here."

Everywhere is dark and eerily quiet; by the time Lucas reaches the edge of town again, it is late into the night. He is physically tired and mentally drained. A dense fog still blankets everything around him.

"It is so late, where could they have gone?" He wonders looking around at the abandoned town.

Not wanting to be found by John again, he attempts to stay hidden in the shadows. Pure exhaustion takes over, and he decides to rest for a few minutes, gather his thoughts, and plan his next move. Sneaking around behind a house looking for an inconspicuous place to rest, he spies a hammock along the back fence nestled in between a couple of trees.

"Perfect I just need fifteen minutes to regain my strength and formulate a plan," Lucas decides as he gets settled into the hammock, and while he tries to think of where his family may have gone, he drifts off to sleep.

Several hours later, as the sun is beginning to rise, Lucas is startled awake by the sound of Kaitlyn screaming his name. He jumps out of the hammock quickly and takes off, running toward the sound. "I can't believe I slept that long, I just wanted a few minutes," he berates himself as he ran.

"Kaitlyn, daddy is coming! Sweetie, where are you?"

Lucas stops and listens for any sound or movement. As he surveys his surroundings, he faintly hears her calling for him again in the distance.

"Daddy, daddy, help me!"

Running as fast as his legs will allow him, he quickly scans his surroundings as he passes by hoping for a glimpse of something that will lead him to his family and out of this nightmare. When he arrives at an abandoned storm basement and hears faint whimpering, he slows down to look carefully. The lock is broken and dangling on the outside of the door. He slowly opens the door and peers inside down the dark stairs cautiously.

"Kaitlyn? Honey, are you down there?"

Lucas is met with total silence. He begins to descend the stairs slowly, keeping his guard up and willing his eyes to adjust to the darkness.

"Kaitlyn," he whispers, descending slowly. "Kaitlyn, baby, where are you?"

Once he reaches the bottom, it is pitch black, and the only light is what is coming from the open door at the top of the stairs from where he just came. With his hands out in front of him he attempts to feel his way around the room, he continues to whisper for his daughter.

Lucas lets out a yelp in pain as he stumbles over something on the ground, and a sharp object slices against the back of his calf. He can feel warm liquid running down into his sock as searing pain shoots up his entire leg. Reaching down to touch the injury, his hand becomes sticky and wet, and he can feel flesh hanging from his wound.

"Daddy!"

Lucas snaps his head up toward the exit as the sound of Brody calling for him from somewhere outside.

"Daddy, where are you?" Brody's voice echoes in Lucas's head as he bounds up the stairs two at a time, exiting the dark basement. Ignoring the burning pain radiating throughout his leg, he presses on toward his son.

Stopping for a moment to get his bearings and let his eyes readjust to the light, he whips his head from side to side, trying to locate where Brody could be; he hears him calling for him again and takes off running in that direction.

"Brody, buddy, say something so I can find you!" Lucas yells, panic dripping from his voice.

"Daddy, over here!"

Lucas, pumped full of adrenaline, no longer feels the pain from his leg and runs faster than he has ever run in his life. He stops short when he arrives at an old, run-down, abandoned playground. A single swing was slowly swaying without a rider, creaking as it went back and forth mocking Lucas.

Spinning in a circle looking at everything around him he

begins to get dizzy and grabs a hold of a metal pole to steady himself as he frantically listens for his son's voice.

"ABIGAIL? Brody, Madison, Kaitlyn? Where are you?" he yells as he falls to his knees and begins screaming in frustration. Pounding his fists on the ground in a fit of rage, he doesn't hear as John slowly approaches behind him.

"This is very unbecoming of you, Lucas."

"You! Where the hell is my family? If you have hurt any of them, I can promise you I will end you and it will not be a quick death," Lucas fumes as he turns his face toward John in pure rage.

"Oh, please. Your family is fine, and you and I both know you are not going to do anything to me. Now get up and let's go. I told you that you wouldn't be leaving yet, I'm not finished with you yet."

"What? I am not going anywhere with you!"

"You most certainly are; if you want to ever see your family again, that is."

"Where are they?" Lucas asks while he slowly pulls himself up to his feet, wincing in pain as he adjusts his weight off his injured leg.

"I told you they are safe; I am not here to hurt your family. You are the only one that can do that. Now, let's go. We need to bandage up that leg." John says as he turns toward the road and begins walking away. "You know the iPad is still in your room. You can check on them yourself once you get back in there," he continues over his shoulder.

Lucas watches on as John walks away from him.

*Should I run? Where would I run to? Everything is oddly aban-doned, and I don't have a car to take me anywhere anymore. How will I find Abigail and the kids? Where are all the people in this town that were here yesterday? It's almost as if I am somehow in a different dimension. That's ridiculous, focus, Lucas. Okay, if I go with him, at least I can see that they are alright. Formulate a plan.*

*Maybe I can figure out what he wants with me and get us all away from him safely; at this point, I don't really see what other option I have.*

Lucas has so many thoughts running through his mind at the same time, he begins to get a headache. Deciding the only course of action is to go back with John so he can verify the safety of his family and create a new game plan, he follows behind him in silence as they walk back toward the magic shop. By the time they reach the store, Lucas is limping and in serious pain. His sock is soaked, and his shoe feels sloshy.

"I will get you a new pair of socks and a bandage after you get settled back in. I'll also bring you in some food." John offers as he holds open the door to his store, ushering Lucas inside.

"How very generous of you." Lucas murmurs as he walks past John and back into his prison.

Thirty minutes later, after dressing the wound on Lucas's leg, John hands him a fresh pair of slipper socks and moves to sit on the only chair in the dark room. Lucas is sitting on the edge of the bed, sadly looking down at his family on the tablet. Abigail is talking with police officers at the rental cabin surrounded by Benjamin and Allison.

"When did Benjamin and Allison get down here? I should have stayed there and waited; we could be on our way out of here right now," he mumbles to himself.

"No, you wouldn't," John states flatly while watching Lucas.

"Please, just let me out of here. My family needs me. They are devastated."

"Are they? Do you honestly think that they are devastated? Why should I let you out of here, Lucas?"

"Why not? You can't even tell me why you are keeping me here in the first place. What do you want from me?" Lucas asks angrily.

"I don't want anything from you, Lucas. I am not the one that put you in here."

"What does that even mean? Who put me in here then? What do I have to do to get out of here?"

"Lucas, let me ask you something, do you think you are a good man? A good husband and father?" John asks, rising from his seat.

Lucas looks back at his captor with a blank expression.

"Yes, of course. Everything I did, everything I do is for my family. I am a great husband and an incredible father," he replies with confidence.

"Do you think your family would agree?"

"Yes, I know they would, my family loves me! Just look at them, they are freaking out. Why are you asking me such stupid questions? Just tell me why you are keeping me here?" Lucas yells before smashing his fist on the wall next to him.

"You are going to remain here until the time in which you are let free," John smirks.

"You are an idiot."

Lucas looks back down to the tablet, watching his family, and when he looks back up, John is again gone. Sitting on the table is an overflowing plate of food. He hadn't realized how hungry he was until he saw the plate. Eating slowly, he continues to watch his family and tries to figure out a way to convince John to let him go free. "It would help if I knew why he was keeping me in here in the first place!" He murmurs to himself, focusing on his wife as she cries.

# CHAPTER 11

"*I* am going to go call Tony," Madison says quietly as they all walk back into the cabin defeated and tired. After spending all day with the search party looking for Lucas, they have still come up empty-handed.

Abigail nods to her daughter before going to sit with Kaitlyn and Brody on the sofa. Brody leans on his mother's chest and hugs her tightly. Abigail looks over at her friends who have joined them in the living room and offers a small smile.

"What if they don't find him, Mommy?" Brody asks.

"We just can't think like that. Okay!" she whispers, exasperated.

Brody and Kaitlyn sadly nod their heads and look over to the tv. The group of them sit quietly, absently watching whatever is on.

"Daddy is gone," Brody says sadly. "The policeman told you that he didn't want us anymore and he ran away."

Benjamin comes over and kneels in front of Brody and firmly states, "Well, that policeman doesn't know your Daddy. You and I both know that he would never do that!"

The adults jump up from their seats and run toward the

front door when they hear footsteps coming up the stairs outside. Hoping to find Lucas, Abigail flings open the door. But, instead, it is Officer Jason and another gentleman dressed in a suit. Obvious disappointment shows across all their faces, but none more than Abigail.

"I wanted to introduce you to Detective Hart. He is going to take over the investigation into the disappearance of your husband," Officer Jason says as he motions to the man standing next to him in the doorway.

"Good evening, Mrs. Ferguson. I am sorry to have to meet you under these circumstances. I see you have guests."

"Yes, these are our friends, Allison and Benjamin."

"How nice, do you mind if we come in? I have a few questions," the detective asks.

Abigail moves to the side, nodding her head and motioning for them to come in. They smile appreciatively and make their way into the living room and stand behind the sofa.

"I am just going to go ahead and get started with my questions if you don't mind. No sense beating around the bush am I right? After all a lot of time has already passed and we all know time is of the essence in cases like this. Were you and your husband having any marital problems Mrs. Ferguson?"

Abigail lets out a loud and frustrated sigh before responding. "No, as I have already stated multiple times, my husband worked too much, and I felt like he was neglecting us because of it, so that caused a few arguments. Nothing drastic or dramatic. I just want him to come home safe and soon."

"Yes, of course, we all want that as well. Do you know of anyone that would be out to hurt Mr. Ferguson?" the detective continues, looking into her eyes.

"What? No, I can't think of anyone that would even consider hurting him. Lucas is a very good man," she responds, shocked at the allegation.

"The entire community knows him, he works with charities,

and is always willing to lend a hand. He is a well-respected man," Benjamin offers from the couch.

Abigail looks at him and smiles. "Thank you for saying that, Ben. He is a very respected man in our community."

"He was a criminal defense attorney, is that right?" Detective Hart questions while glancing down at a notebook he has in his hand.

"He *is* a defense attorney, yes," she corrects. "Please do not speak about my husband in the past tense."

"I apologize. Did he seem worried or anxious about anything or anyone?" he presses.

"No, he just seemed busy. Like always."

"Do you mind if I look around your cabin? It won't take long."

"We have only been here one day; I am not sure what you think you will find, but sure, be my guest," she responds, shrugging.

Detective Hart motions for Jason to stay with Abigail and her guests while he walks toward the kitchen. They could hear shuffling and items being moved throughout the cabin. Abigail sits down on the couch and glances over at Jason who is standing by the door waiting patiently. Allison and Benjamin sit with Abigail, each having a hand placed in comfort and support on her leg.

After a few minutes, Detective Hart returns with a prescription bottle, a shirt, and a pair of shorts in his hand. Mrs. Ferguson, could you tell me about these pills, please?"

Abigail walks over to the detective and reaches out for the bottle; she looks at him surprised and shrugs her shoulders.

"They are his sleeping pills. He has a prescription for them. You can tell right on the bottle that it is current."

"There seem to be quite a few missing, though," he replies, eyeing her suspiciously.

She looks back at him, surprised and confused. "What do

you mean? He took a couple extra pills every now and then when he still couldn't sleep. He was going to go to the doctor and discuss getting the dose increased, but he hadn't gotten around to it yet."

"So, you are saying he took the missing pills?" he questions skeptically.

"Yes, of course. What else do you think happened to them?" she asks, dumbfounded.

Detective Hart continues to stand there looking back and forth between the bottle and Abigail.

"Can you explain these items of clothing that were found in your bathroom that appear to have blood on them?"

"Of course, Brody got hit in the face with a football on our way into town and he got a little bit of his blood on me."

"How did he get hit?" Detective Hart asks raising an eyebrow suspiciously.

"Well, Lucas was trying to play with him and tossed it at him thinking he would catch it, only he didn't. It smacked him in the face," Abigail answered frustrated and defensive.

Detective Hart looked over to Brody and examined his face carefully.

"Did your daddy hit you son?"

"Wait a minute, he didn't HIT him! It was an accident, with a ball!" She shouted panicked realizing where this questioning was headed.

Ignoring the mother, the detective took a step closer to Brody and continued. "Has your daddy ever hurt you like this before? It's okay, you can tell me."

Brody glanced at his mother and back to the detective before looking down at his hands sadly. "No, my daddy doesn't really ever play with me."

"I see," the detective replied turning his attention back to Abigail who was staring at Brody with a tear in her eye.

"Did you give Lucas those extra pills, Mrs. Ferguson?" he demands.

"I'm sorry, what?" She shrieks.

The detective stands there with his lips pressed in a firm line waiting for a response from Abigail.

Allison and Benjamin jump to their feet and stand next to Abigail protectively.

"Are you kidding me right now? Is that a real question? How does that work in your head? Are my kids in on it too? Like I gave Lucas drugs and then what? We were in a store; then *he* wasn't. I was with the kids the *entire* time! Do I look like I could dispose of a *body*? I mean, seriously, what in the actual hell are you even saying? *This* is what you have come up with? *This* is what makes sense to you?" Abigail screams as she throws the prescription bottle across the room angrily.

"You are way out of line and even farther off base. That is not even remotely possible!" Allison says, defending her friend. "The idea is beyond stupid."

"I can't believe you would even waste your time asking such ridiculous questions," Benjamin chimes in. "That absolutely makes no sense. Are there any actual trained officers that we can put onto this case? Because it seems to me that from the moment you guys started working this case you have been chasing all the wrong leads and wasting a whole lot of time!"

"That is the problem sir, there are no leads," Jason informs from his post at the door.

"Maybe if you spent time looking for them instead of coming up here accusing an innocent and scared woman, you would find some!" Benjamin lashes back putting a protective arm around Abigail.

Holding his hands up in defense, the detective takes a step back. "Well, actually it does make sense to me, and things like that happen quite often, actually. However, I do not necessarily think that is the case here. I do have to ask all the questions, though. I can assure you that I am going to find your husband."

"I hope you do. If there is nothing else you need from me, I am going to have to ask you to leave and get back to finding him," Abigail responds through gritted teeth as she walks over, and flings open the front door.

"Here is my card; if you think of anything else that could be helpful, give me a call. Otherwise, I will be in touch with you as soon as I know anything. My team specializes in missing persons. We will find out what happened to your husband one way or the other," Detective Hart says as he hands Abigail the card, and he and Officer Jason turn to leave.

Abigail stares after them as they drive away with both worry and anger. "*Oh, how I wish I could just wake up from this nightmare.*"

Closing the door and laying her head up against it she lets out a soft sigh.

"Mommy?" Kaitlyn calls from her place on the sofa.

Standing straight and looking over at her two youngsters she offers a small smile. "I am okay, why don't you guys go get ready for bed and you can watch tv for a few minutes."

The two slowly got up and walked toward the bedroom while Abigail took a deep breath and looked at Allison sadly. "I am so sorry you guys had to come all the way down here to help me deal with this, but I am so grateful," she sighs as tears begin to fall down her cheeks once again. "I don't know what to do, and I am so thankful that I am not dealing with this on my own."

"You know we would do anything for you honey," Allison says comfortingly. "We will figure this out, somehow."

Nodding back at her best friend she walks toward her bedroom. "I am going to go take a bath and try to calm down," Abigail says, walking to the bathroom. "If anything happens, come get me."

"Of course, sweetie, go relax, we will watch the kids," Allison says, hugging her friend.

Inside the large bathroom Abigail fills up the garden tub and lays her head back. Sheer mental exhaustion bearing down on her. Staring at the ceiling with tears streaming down her face, she whispers, "I love you, Lucas, please come back to me."

# CHAPTER 12

The following morning, Abigail wakes up in a pool of sweat. She spent the entire night having nightmare after nightmare about what could possibly have happened to her husband. After all of that tossing and turning, she still felt exhausted but knew she would not be getting any more sleep today. So, she flings her legs over the side of the bed, grabs her robe, and quietly makes her way into the living room, where Ben is sitting on the couch watching the local news.

"Hey, did you get any sleep?" he questions, "No offense, but you still don't look too good."

"None taken. I slept, but not well. I realize that I look and feel like total crap, but until we find Lucas, I don't see that changing."

"Abby, what can I do?" Allison asks, concern for her best friend evident across her face as she walks out of her bedroom into the living room wrapping her arms around Benjamin's neck and kissing his temple softly.

"I don't even know what to do, honestly. I don't know what to think; I don't even know what to say to the kids. Where is he?" she cries.

"I don't know, honey," she responds, rubbing her friend's shoulder.

"At this point, is it too much to hope that he is even still alive? How could he be surviving without any money? Without anybody seeing him literally anywhere? Just gone without a trace?" Abigail questions quietly.

"I wish I had the words to say, but honestly, Abby, I just don't know," Allison says as she reaches over and grabs her friends' hands and squeezes them in support.

"This is all just too much," Abigail murmurs softly to no one in particular as she wipes a lone tear from her cheek.

"Mom," Madison cries as tears stream down her face, running toward out of the bedroom towards Abigail, holding her cell phone.

"Hey, hey, it is going to be okay," Abigail says trying to calm her eldest daughter.

Mom, Tony just called me, somehow the kids from school found out about dad. There is now a rumor going around school saying daddy went crazy and ran away from us."

"What? How would anyone back at home know anything about Lucas being missing? What in the world is happening? Madison honey, they are being immature, dumb, and dramatic; just stay off your phone for a little while! Tell Tony not to tell you things like that, it is entirely unhelpful."

Abigail reaches for her daughter and pulls her into a comforting hug, letting her cry on her shoulder.

"Why mom?"

"Do you think Daddy is dead, Mommy?" Brody asks through his tears as he makes his first appearance of the morning. Slowly wandering into the living room still groggy and visibly upset.

"No, baby, no. I don't, but I do think we are going to find him! There are a lot of people looking. In fact, Allison, Benjamin, and I were just about to plan for how we were going to find Daddy today! You guys go get dressed and I will get some breakfast together so we can get out there and get the day started!" she requests, trying to put on a brave face for her children.

Madison and Brody head back toward the bedroom to get ready and Abigail walks toward the kitchen. "Here, let me help you honey," Allison says as she follows behind her friend.

Standing over the stove, staring at an empty pan Abigail finds herself unable to cook breakfast. She begins crying uncontrollably and grips the counter to steady herself before her knees give out. Allison grabbed her by the shoulders and led her toward the dining room table and helped her sit down.

"Sit here, let me take care of breakfast."

"It's like I am living a bad dream. I keep expecting to wake up and for things to be back to normal, but I am not waking up." Abigail solemnly says staring off into space.

"You can only do what you can do, Abigail. You are doing the best you can in the circumstances you have been given," Benjamin responds softly, walking into the kitchen to see if he can help with anything.

"Am I? Because it feels like I am failing my kids, I don't know what to say to them. Their questions are valid, and I have no answers for them. At this point I can't imagine where Lucas could be, why he hasn't gotten a hold of us."

"Abby, I can't imagine what I would do in your situation, you are so strong, and you are out here fighting to find Lucas. You are allowed to have your feelings, cry, scream, worry, get angry just don't give up." Allison says as she places a glass of orange juice in front of her.

A short time later, everyone is sitting around the table eating the breakfast Allison and Benjamin prepared and are chatting about nothing deep or important. All the adults want to keep the mood light before they head out for another day of searching.

"It's nice not having any phones at the table," Kaitlyn says observantly.

Abigail looks around the table and realizes that she is right, no one has their phones, not even Madison. "It *is* pretty nice; it gives us the ability to just talk, and pay attention to each other," Abigail responds with a small smile for her daughter. "Madison, honey, I was thinking, how do you feel about switching to distance learning, kind of like homeschooling? Just for a little while?"

"I don't know, Mom. I mean, I hate the kids at that stupid school, but homeschool?" she replies with a twisted look on her face.

"Just for a little while, until everything gets sorted out and calmed down, and it isn't really homeschooling, you will still do all the work from your school just not there," her mother says reassuringly. "I don't want you to fall behind on your studies while we are down here. You can do everything online. Once we get back home, whenever that is, you may not want to go back right away, and this will give you flexibility without getting behind."

"Can I homeschool too? David still picks his nose and eats his buggers. It's disgusting," Kaitlyn asks with a grimace.

"I think it would be a good idea for all of you to do distance learning for a little bit," Abigail states with confidence.

"But when will I even have time to worry about schoolwork? I will be helping you guys look for Dad, then once we find him, we are going to go back home."

"I think it would be helpful if you could stay here with your siblings while we are out searching. It will be easier for us to work on finding daddy out there if I am not worried about you guys at the same time. You could work on your schoolwork while you are here," Abigail explains slowly hoping that her daughter doesn't freak out on her plan.

"Yea. Sure. Fine, whatever you say, Mom." Madison replies obviously upset but choosing to let it go for now.

Abigail looks relieved and exhales the breath she didn't realize she had been holding as she grabs her mug of coffee and slowly brings it to her lips.

"Okay, great, now that we have all of that straightened out, we should probably go ahead and get going and head into town. Let's get an update from the search parties and go from there," Benjamin chimes in as he stands to gather his things.

"You guys behave, stay inside, and try not to fight with each other while we are gone, okay?"

"Sure mom, don't worry about us, we will be fine." Madison responds flatly.

"Listen honey, I know you don't want to stay here, but I appreciate you helping me out with Kaitlyn and Brody. I am proud of you and love you very much."

Madison nods at her mother and walks toward the bedroom quietly.

"They will be okay Abigail, you ready to go?" Allison asks putting her arm around Abigail gently.

"Not really, but let's go."

The trio walks out of the cabin and load up into Benjamin's truck before heading into town ready to find Lucas.

Thirty minutes later, Abigail, Benjamin, and Allison arrive back in town and look through the crowd of volunteers for Detective Hart, hoping for some kind of an update. They pull over and park when they see him standing outside the town square, talking with a couple of volunteers wearing orange vests. Abigail hops out of the truck and walks up to him quickly.

"Pardon the interruption, but Detective Hart, have you found out anything new regarding Lucas?"

"No, ma'am. Like I said before, there are no clues anywhere. If I didn't know any better, I would say he was never even here."

Okay, well, my friends and I are here to help. What areas are you guys focusing on today?" She asks stranding tall, putting on a brave face.

"There is a team going up the ridge right over there in about fifteen minutes. You can join them. That particular area has not yet been searched, so we are going to be having most of the teams working on scouring that area today."

"Okay, we will be ready to leave when they are."

Detective Hart taps one of the volunteers on the shoulder and motions for him to alert the lead point man that Abigail, Benjamin, and Lucas would be joining his team this morning. Immediately the guy runs off, and the detective turns his attention to Abigail and studies her intently for a few seconds.

"How are you holding up?" he questions, nodding in acknowledgement to Benjamin and Allison, who are walking up behind Abigail, standing just a few feet behind her. Close enough to offer support, far enough to offer a small amount of privacy.

"How do you think I am holding up? I am living a real-life nightmare with no way to wake up!"

"That is totally understandable, and I do wish that I had better news for you Abigail." Detective Hart takes a deep breath, running his hands through his hair and continues. "Listen, there is something that I wanted to talk to you about; the prescription Lucas was taking."

"Really? Again! Are you sure that you have done this before because you waste a lot of time following up on absolutely the stupidest crap that does nothing to find my husband!"

"I apologize if I offended you yesterday that was not my intention, I was just doing my job. However, I spoke with a doctor friend of mine, and he verified my initial concern. He informed me that in his professional opinion that if Lucas was abusing his prescription pills like you said he was, then it could and most likely would have easily altered his state of mind."

Abigail stands with her mouth hanging agape. She started to

shake her head slowly, trying to remain calm. Seeing her in distress, Benjamin and Allison got to her side immediately. Reaching for her shoulders instinctively, Benjamin grips her tightly. Recognizing the storm brewing in Abigail's eyes, Allison grabs her friends' hand and squeezes.

"I *never* said he was abusing his medicine; he just took more than he was originally prescribed, and only occasionally. On the really stressful days, he just needed a little extra in order to get to sleep. The prescribed dose wasn't working properly anymore. He hadn't had a chance to get back in to see the doctor about increasing his dose yet," she argues back while shooting daggers from her eyes.

"Well, whether you accept it or not, *that is* abusing them, Mrs. Ferguson," he forcefully replies. "And the fact of the matter is, the medicine he was taking has a common side effect that adjusts and changes rational thinking when not taken as prescribed."

"I was with my husband every single day. At no point was he irrational! He wasn't abusing the medicine, and his doctor would have increased his dosage as soon as he was able to go in anyway. This stupid story you keep trying to feed me about my husband abusing his prescription is not going to get you anywhere. You are constantly wasting time and helping no one. My husband is out there somewhere, and I can guarantee he did not just leave us! Did we have our issues? Yes, but would he just abandon his family? Hell no! So just STOP! Unless you have anything to say to me that could actually help in finding my husband, then I am going to have to say goodbye; as I am going to go out there and do something productive in the search for him!"

Abigail grabs hold of Allison's hand and turns to walk away. Benjamin shakes his head in frustration at the detective before following closely behind his wife and friend. However, they did not get far before they heard Detective Hart clear his throat and drop a bombshell on them.

"Listen, I was clear with you from the very beginning, I am going to be following all angles and leads and do whatever I have to do to find Lucas. Before you go though, I do have one more question for you. Did you know about the offshore savings account your husband had been stocking money away into?"

Abigail stops in her tracks, drops Allison's hand, and slowly turns back to face Detective Hart with a completely blank face. Surely, she did not hear him right. Benjamin looks over at Allison, both stunned into silence and shakes his head in disbelief.

"I'm sorry, the what?"

"I am assuming by the look on your face, you did not know about this account. Which means that you also did not know that it currently has a balance of close to three-quarters of a million dollars in it."

Abigail stares at Detective Hart, utter confusion appearing on her face. She takes an unsteady step toward Benjamin. Placing her hands on her cheeks she begins to shake her head in her hands, unsure of what to say or how to even process this shocking and new information. Finally, she looks at her friends and grabs ahold of Benjamin's arm, afraid her legs will give out at any moment. Benjamin leads her to a bench nearby and guides her to sit. She is visibly shaking throughout her entire body.

"Is it possible that maybe you didn't know your husband as well as you thought you did, Mrs. Ferguson?" He asks coolly before turning to walk away.

Abigail stares blankly out into space unable to wrap her mind around what Detective Hart told her. How could Lucas have an account with nearly a million dollars in it. What was he doing with it? How long had he had it? How could he have not told her?

Allison snaps Abigail out of her inner thoughts as she drops down on the bench next to her. "Abby, did you know about that money?"

Abigail just shakes her head no and then leans into Allison. Her body continuing to shake uncontrollably as so many conflicting thoughts raced through her mind at once.

"Allison, how is that possible?" Abigail questions as she once again begins to cry.

"You guys ready over there?" a volunteer yells toward the trio, motioning to the search party gathering at the base of the ridge that they are about to climb and search.

"Yes, we are coming," Allison yells back, grabbing hold of Abigail's hand and helping her to her feet.

Abigail looks over at the ridge quietly before turning her tear-filled eyes to her friends and whispering sadly. "I don't think we are going to find him up there, you guys. I don't know if I still believe he is going to ever come back home after all."

Benjamin wraps his arm around her shoulders as they walk toward the group, allowing her to cry into his arm; having no words of encouragement after the encounter with the detective, they all continue to walk along together in silence.

*"Maybe none of us actually knew him the way we thought we did,"* he thinks to himself sadly.

# CHAPTER 13

"ell, now you sure are full of surprises, aren't you?" John admonishes Lucas as they watch the iPad, referring to the explosive revelation from Detective Hart to Abigail about the secret bank account.

"Oh, shut up! You think you know so much; you absolutely know nothing! That was not anything sinister or sneaky," Lucas defends. "It was going to be a surprise for when I retired. The only reason I didn't tell her about it was because I was pretending like I didn't even have it. My goal was to get it up to a million dollars and ignore it until the kids were grown and I retired. I wanted to use it to travel all over with Abigail."

"Why couldn't you tell her about it then?" John asks, doubtful.

"Because if I told her about it, then it would be something tangible we would have to discuss and would always be in the back of our minds. I didn't want it to be something we could spend on a whim. Like I said, I treated it like I didn't even have it."

"That is one of the problems with families today, always thinking about the future, but forgetting to live in the moment.

Sure, you should plan for the future, but what if tomorrow never comes? You wasted all that time preparing for something you'll never even have missing out on the moments that you could have. Makes me wonder, do you have any other secrets you've been hiding from your wife, Lucas?" John questions with his eyes raised.

"No," he answers sullenly while getting lost in deep thought. "All of these little things I did for Abigail, you and those idiot officers are twisting around turning them into something that they aren't and making me look bad."

"*We* are making you look bad? You don't think that your lying and your own actions of ignoring your family regularly is what makes you look bad?" John questions while rolling his eyes. "How about some personal accountability."

"That is exactly what I am talking about. It was a good thing I was doing, saving up money to surprise my wife and travel the world with her. However, you have turned it around and made it seem like I was doing something shady. Like I was stealing or going to sneak off with another woman. That just isn't true."

"Whatever, helps you sleep at night, my friend."

"We are not friends! You are a total lunatic. When I get out of here and believe me, I *will* get out of here, I am going to make sure you speed the rest of your life is prison for the crimes you are committing here!"

"Hahahahaha, you are a funny guy. Unfortunately, I think your lack of sleep may be getting to your brain. At this rate, you are never going to get out of here!"

Lucas gazes down at the tablet on the table and places his finger on Abigail's face softly. "Yes, I will."

Lucas looks up quickly with pure rage displayed across his face. "What is wrong with you? Why are you such a total psychopath? You are keeping me away from my family for absolutely no reason whatsoever! When I ask you what you want from me you talk in riddles. Just do what you are going to do and quit playing all these games!"

John stares at Lucas and lets him rant. Then, when he is finished, he begins to question him.

"Did you happen to notice how much your family enjoyed eating at the table with no electronics? Almost as if they craved that attention and time," John prods with a hint of sarcasm in his voice.

"Work does not stop just because I am eating breakfast, lunch or dinner," Lucas snaps back, rolling his eyes.

"But it could, couldn't it?" John calmly asks, while Lucas stares back at him in silence contemplating what he is saying.

"You do understand that I have a very important job, right? I mean, I literally have the lives of my clients in my hands," Lucas snaps back sarcastically, looking at John like he is the biggest moron he had ever seen. "Why are you having such a hard time realizing this?"

"*You* understand that your clients are criminals, yes?"

"Allegedly," Lucas corrects. "But that doesn't change the fact that their lives are in my hands."

"You are not a doctor Lucas; you can put down your phone and eat dinner with your family without someone dying!" John states firmly. "You really have to fix your priorities."

"My priorities are to take care of my family. Do you have any idea how much our house costs? Cars? All the activities that the kids are in? That takes money! In order to have money, I have to *work*!" Lucas yells back in frustration.

John sits quietly, staring at Lucas while shaking his head for a moment. "Sonny, you still do not get it."

"Get *what*?" he yells back, slamming his hand down onto the table.

"I am not going to tell you! That would defeat the entire point!"

Lucas glares at John for what feels like an hour. "Okay, then why don't you tell me, what is the POINT?"

Letting out a long sigh, John rolls his eyes. "I am not going to tell you that either."

"Then let me go!"

"I already told you, I am not the one keeping you here; I am just keeping an eye on you while you are here," John responds, shrugging his shoulders.

"Well, then who *is* keeping me? Why? What do they want?" Lucas pleads.

"All good questions, none of which I can answer for you right now. Just focus on your family; they will be the ones to ultimately get you through this."

"I don't understand you, man. You are creepy as hell and refuse to give any kind of a real response!" Lucas fires back. "How do I get a straight answer from you?"

Lucas has so much rage building up inside him that he explodes, swinging at John, catching him off guard. His fist connects with the jaw of his captor, causing John to lose his balance, landing with a hard thud onto the floor. Lucas takes this opportunity to tackle the older man and continue his tirade of punches. However, even though John is much older than Lucas, he is very physically fit. He is able to maneuver his way out from under him. They both wrestled for a few minutes before John could get back onto his feet. Finally, he violently shoves Lucas away from him and onto the bed.

"Now, I already told you once that we were not going to be doing that!"

"You are a freaking psycho. If you are going to kill me, then get it over with. If not, then let me out of here. You aren't just torturing me; you are torturing my family!

"I am not doing anything."

"Why do you think you have no responsibility in any of this? You are the one keeping me held captive. Even if you were not the mastermind behind my abduction, you are the one standing in here now, not letting me go! You are complicit in this crime, and yes, this is a crime!"

"Putting your work above your family should be considered a crime as well."

"Are you kidding me? I never said my work was more important than my family," Lucas says defensively. "And even if I did, that is nowhere near the same as kidnapping a grown man and holding him against his will. All while torturing him by forcing him to watch his family cry in his absence!"

"You don't have to say it; your actions say it for you."

"You are so frustrating. You have no idea what my job entails! If I am not prepared for my cases, I could lose my law license. I cannot just hang out at home doing nothing and then show up to court. That isn't how it works."

"Are you trying to justify your poor choices to yourself or to me?"

"I don't have to justify myself to anyone. I am not out partying or sleeping around with other women. I am working. I take the responsibility of my job very seriously. You calling anything I do poor choices is rich seeing as how you are a lunatic kidnapper."

"Your name-calling does not hurt my feelings, nor does it do anything to get you out of here any faster. What about the responsibility of your family? Shouldn't they be your highest priority? Why are you so concerned with keeping your law license but not concerned with keeping your family?"

"Have you not been listening to anything I have said? I don't want to keep having this same argument with you. Just tell me what you or whoever is keeping me in here want, and I promise, it is done! No questions asked."

John reaches over, slaps Lucas across the face, and scowls at him.

"*You* are the one that isn't listening!"

Lucas jumps to his feet, ready to fight again. Shoving John in the chest with all his might, he watches as the older man goes flying backward, slamming into the wall.

John, momentarily stunned, pounds his fist onto his chest to catch his breath and then stands up straight and tall in a show of dominance. Flinging his head from side to side, causing it to crack, then rolling his shoulders, he squares up in front of Lucas, puffing out his chest.

"Feel better? Because you most certainly will not get that chance again."

"I won't feel better until I get out of here, away from you and back to my work and family!"

"Then I suggest you start paying closer attention," John snaps right before he pulls his arm back, punching Lucas across the temple sending him flailing back onto the bed in an awkward position.

Knocked out cold, John rearranges Lucas on the bed into a more comfortable position before exiting the room through the trick wall.

"I warned him, that idiot really doesn't listen."

# CHAPTER 14

*L*ucas stirs awake and looks up at the ceiling. Moving his head from side to side, he takes in his surroundings. Then, jolting up in the bed as the realization hits him, he is back in his bed, at his house.

"What in the worst nightmare ever was that?" He questions to himself as he rises out of his bed, running his hands through his hair in an attempt to rid himself of that awful dream.

"Abigail? Honey where are you?" He calls while getting out of bed and walking toward the bedroom door. He can hear talking coming from down the hall. He glances over at the clock on the nightstand and jumps in surprise at the time. "Are you serious? I have never slept past noon in my entire life! I must be getting sick!"

Opening the bedroom door and exiting out into the living room he sees Abigail and the kids sitting on the sofa watching tv together. An overwhelming sense of relief floods him as he rushes toward them and drops down to his knees in front of Abigail.

"Baby, you have no idea how good it is to see your face and know that you and the kids are alright. You would not believe the awful dream I had. I also think I may be coming down with something, I should probably check my temperature. I can't believe I slept in like that."

Abigail does not respond to her husband, instead she continues to watch the television, ignoring everything Lucas has just said to her.

"Hello, Abigail? Are you mad at me or something? Honey? I am sorry for whatever, can you just talk to me?" Lucas pleads looking up at his wife who is acting as if he is not even there.

He glances over at his children that are all so engulfed in whatever movie they are watching on the T.V. that none of them acknowledge his presence either.

"Okay you guys, this is just plain rude! What is everyone's problem today?" he questions looking from face to face for some type of response. But receives nothing.

Suddenly the front door opens and Lucas watches as he walks in the front door face down staring at his phone.

"Hey babe, how did your meeting go?" Abigail questions to the Lucas that just waltzed in the front door, however, he offers her no reply. Instead, he sits down on the accent chair and continues to type onto his phone.

"Typical," she mumbles turning her attention back to the movie in front of her.

"What is happening?" Lucas wonders as he stares at himself from the floor in front of his wife. He gently places his head on her lap and closes his eyes only to open them when the feeling of warmth engulfs his entire body.

Lifting his head up he realizes he is now sitting outside at the picnic table in their backyard. Looking around he sees Abigail hugging Brody who is crying by the swing set. He jumps up to his feet and runs toward them wanting to know that everything is okay.

"He promised mom, he said he would show up and he didn't. I was the only kid in the whole class who didn't have a parent there for career day! Why didn't he show up? Why doesn't he care about me?" Brody sobbed into Abigail's embrace.

"Oh sweetie, he does care about you. I am so sorry he was not there; I am sure something just came up at the office."

"Something always comes up at the office," he argued.

"Brody, buddy, I love you so much. I am sorry, please forgive me," Lucas begs, all the while Abigail and Brody do not see or hear him.

Lucas began walking backwards toward the house watching as Abigail continues to console their son.

"This is not real, this is not happening," Lucas mutters to himself. "I must be having a nervous breakdown of some sort," Lucas continues as he walks in the backdoor into the kitchen where Abigail is drinking a glass of wine with Allison while sitting at the counter chatting.

"So, what are you going to do hon?" Allison asks while looking at her friend sadly.

"Honestly, I have no idea, I still love him so much and I want this to work, but I cannot see myself living like this for the rest of my life."

"I understand, whatever you need, you know that I am always here for you! Just don't make any rash decisions." Allison offers while placing her hand on top of Abigail's reassuringly.

"I know, you are an incredible friend. I don't know what I would do without you honestly."

"The same thing I would do without you, go insane," Allison laughs while leaning over and hugging her friend tightly.

"This is not happening, this is not happening, this is not happening, "Lucas begins to chant as he starts to slam his head against the wall willing to get out of this awful loop of whatever version of his life this is. I am not a bad guy, I don't understand why no one can see that I love my family and work hard so they can have the best life possible. Why is this happening? With one final slam of his head Lucas drops to the floor unconscious.

# CHAPTER 15

*L*ater that evening, everyone is gathered back at the cabin, eating dinner around the table quietly. Abigail is fighting tears and cannot stop thinking about the secret bank account that Lucas had been hiding from her.

"Brody, do you want to play baseball this year?" Allison asks in between bites of her food. She is attempting to keep the conversation away from Lucas for the sake of the kids.

"No, I am not very good. Daddy was supposed to help me before the season started; I don't want the other kids to make fun of me," he replies sadly.

"I can help you get better, buddy! I played baseball when I was a kid, and not to toot my own horn but I was pretty dang good too," Benjamin says enthusiastically.

"You would help me?"

"Sure, kiddo! It will be fun!"

Abigail looks over at Benjamin with gratitude. "I am not sure what I did to deserve such great friends, but I can tell you this, I am so incredibly thankful that I have you. That my kids have you."

"You would do the same for us Abigail. This is what friends are for. Brody, we can get started after dinner big guy!"

"Can we, Mom? Can we?" Brody asks with a huge smile.

"Yes, of course you can honey," she smiles back.

"Thank you, Ben. You have no idea what this means to me," she whispers to him. "I don't know how I will ever repay you and Allison for all your help during all this."

"You will never have to know; we will always be here for you, anything you need!" Allison says while squeezing her friends' hand gently.

"Okay, Mommy, I am all done. Can we go play now?" Brody interrupts excitedly. Abigail looks over at his still full plate, over half of his food completely untouched. She gives him a smirk, knowing he is just excited to get outside and play ball.

"You sure you are done, honey? You may be hungry later if you don't eat some more of that."

"I'll be fine; I won't be hungry promise. Please, Mom?" Brody pleads.

"You can go ahead and go outside and get warmed up; Benjamin will meet you out there when he is done," Abigail laughs back. "But put your plate on the counter, you are definitely going to be hungry later!"

Taking one last big bite of his food, Benjamin looks over to Brody and smiles. "I am coming, big guy. Food can wait."

"*Yeah!*"

Later that evening, Abigail looks through the kitchen window and washes the dishes. Watching Brody playing with Benjamin and Allison is sitting on a deck chair braiding Kaitlyn's hair, while Madison sits nearby, presumably texting Tony. Her heart gets a pang of sadness as she misses Lucas and longs for these moments with her husband.

"I can't believe he would leave us," she whispers to herself sadly as she finishes cleaning up the kitchen.

Several hours later Abigail has tucked the kids into bed and is silently watching them sleep while clutching one of Lucas's shirts to her chest. Allison walks up behind Abigail in the bedroom putting her hand on her shoulder offering her a half smile. "I can smell him on this shirt," Abigail sighs.

"I am so sorry, Abby," the friend offers in consolation.

"Do you think Lucas could have run away from us? I never thought our problems were that bad. I always thought they could be fixed. I just wanted him to spend more time with us, work less, make us a priority you know. I couldn't have ever imagined he would run out on his family like this."

"A week ago, I would have said no way, Lucas has always been a stand-up guy. Sure, he worked too much, but that isn't a crime. I have to say, though, it is really odd how he had almost a million dollars saved in an account you knew nothing about. Why? I just cannot wrap my head around it. And how is there just no sign of him anywhere?"

"I know, me either. What was he doing with it? Why would he not have told me about it?"

A loud knock on the front door makes them jump in surprise. Abigail runs to it and flings the door open, only to see Detective Hart once again. He has come alone this time, his hands are laced together in front of him, and he has a solemn look on his face.

"Do you have anything worthwhile to say to me? Or are you here to sling more absurd accusations" Abigail asks, her voice laced with anger and frustration.

"I don't know how worthwhile you will find it, but I do have something I need to discuss with you this evening, and it is important."

Abigail opens the door and leads him into the living room, motioning for him to sit.

"Mrs. Ferguson, I really am sorry for all that you have been going through these last couple of days. However, with that being said I do have to be honest with you; we have decided to close the investigation into your husband's disappearance. There are no charges to be filed against you or anyone else for that matter. We have come to this conclusion based on the fact that there is no evidence of foul play and no evidence of any type of crime. There is just no evidence, period," he attempts to explain to a shocked Abigail.

"So, what exactly do you think happened to him? I mean, he didn't just disappear! I need your help; my kids need their father to come home!"

"Mrs. Ferguson, our final conclusion is that he ran away of his own free will," he states matter-of-factly.

Feeling her legs becoming weak, she feared her knees would buckle. Consequently, Abigail stumbled to the couch and sits down in shock while staring at the detective in pure disbelief.

"You think he just left? Just left his wife of over a decade and his 3 children? Without a word? Just left his law practice that he spent day and night building and working? Just walked away from everything. He would not do that!"

"I understand that this is hard to hear; but there are hundreds of cases just like this one all over the country. The missing person usually turns up on a beach in another country somewhere. They just get burnt out and snap. It has nothing to do with you or your kids. Something inside of him probably just cracked under the pressure of his life. Like I said earlier, it could have had something to do with the medicine he was taking. He was no longer thinking clearly. He obviously has the monetary means to start a new life," Detective Hart replies with sympathy.

"I am not going to tell my kids that their father just up and left them because he lost his damn mind!" she yells, beginning to have a panic attack.

"I can't tell you what to tell your kids ma'am, that is up to you. I am just informing you of the status of this case from our side."

"But you stood in this same room and promised me that you were going to find him one way or the other!"

"And this is me fulfilling that promise, I have found that he ran away," he defended

"No, no that is not finding him. You must actually find him!" Abigail screamed dropping her head into her hands and screaming crying.

Allison who has been standing in the doorway of the bedroom watching and listening quietly rushes to her friend and drops down onto the couch next to her, grabbing ahold of Abigail and embracing her into a firm hug. Realizing that Abigail was beginning to struggle with her breathing she yelled out for her husband. "Ben, Ben, I need your help." Immediately his footsteps can be heard running across the cabin.

"What's wrong?" he shouts, but then seeing the state of Abigail his stomach drops into his feet. "Did you find him?" He asks panic showing on his usually handsome features.

Allison just shakes her head no and releases her hold on Abigail. Benjamin gently grabs her by her shoulders and carefully lays her down on the couch. Hysterically Abigail begins to cry while turning onto her side and curling up into the fetal position.

"Please, Mrs. Ferguson, you have to breathe. I understand your frustration, but we cannot keep looking for someone with nothing to go on and in a situation in which it seems that they do not want to be found."

"Abigail, what's wrong? Why are you crying?" he asks, looking toward Detective Hart with worry. "What is going on? What did you say to her?"

"They aren't going to look for Lucas anymore," Allison states flatly as she rubs the arm of her friend, trying to calm her down.

"I was just telling Mrs. Ferguson that we are closing the missing person's case for Lucas Ferguson."

"Why? If you haven't found him, why would you stop

looking for him? It has only been a few days." he replies in shock.

Just then, the kids come walking out of the bedroom into the living room dazed and half asleep. The screaming has woken them all up, and the fear is evident across each of their little faces.

"I don't want them to see their mother like this; I will take them back to the bedroom. Let me know if you need me!" Allison whispers to Benjamin, getting up and motioning for the kids to come with her.

"Is my mom okay?" Madison questions. She looks over her shoulder and sees her mother curled up, crying in the fetal position on the couch. Benjamin is kneeling in front of her attempting to block her from the view of the kids.

"She is going to be okay. Let's just give her a few minutes to talk to the detective alone. Okay, guys?"

"Is Daddy dead?" Kaitlyn questions, tears welling up in her eyes.

"No, sweetie, that isn't why he came over. I am sure your mom will talk to you about everything in a little while, okay?"

In the living room, Detective Hart is arguing with Benjamin while he stands over Abigail protectively giving her time to sob on the couch and work through the emotions she must be feeling.

"What do you mean you are not going to look for Lucas anymore. That is literally your job!" Benjamin demands.

"It has been concluded that he left on his own and does not want to be found," Detective Hart states flatly.

"You mean to tell me that you think he actually ran away?"

"That is our final conclusion, yes. Should we be presented with any evidence that proves to the contrary we can always reopen the case."

"Why would anyone leave this family? That doesn't make any sense; there must be another explanation," he argues.

"Do you have one?" Detective Hart asks condescendingly.

"No, again, that is *your* job! But I can tell you that it doesn't make any sense that a man of Lucas's success would just up and leave his entire life with no warning," he argues back.

"It actually happens much more than you realize," Detective Hart replies solemnly.

"Abby, I am so sorry," Benjamin says as he drops back down to his knees, consoling her. "What can I do? Should I go get Allison?"

Abigail begins to sit up on the couch and straightens out her clothing slowly. She takes her hands and wipes her face with purpose, strength, and then takes a long deep breath.

"No, it is fine. We had our problems; I thought we could work them out; I was obviously wrong. My priority now has to be the kids. Making sure that their life is not any more difficult than it has been these last couple of days," she says, trying to portray strength in her voice, even though she was dying inside.

"I will see myself out then, Mrs. Ferguson. I really do hope for the best for you and your family. Good luck," Detective Hart states as he turns to leave.

"Just get out," she replies flatly.

He turns back to her stunned by her outburst but can understand where she is coming from. Quietly he opens the door and exits the cabin.

Abigail and Benjamin both sit in silence on the couch. Abigail looks off into the distance while concentrating on her breathing.

"What are you going to do?" Benjamin asks after a few minutes.

"I don't know," she replies slowly. "But I know that I need to talk to the kids. This is going to change their whole world. How could Lucas do this to them? I mean, if he didn't want to be with me anymore, I could learn to accept that, but the kids. This is so unfair to them!"

"Do you want me to get Allison and give you guys some alone time?" Benjamin asks, worried.

"No, please stay. I think I may need the moral support from you both, the kids too. I don't know how we are going to get through this," she replies, gripping his arm tightly.

"The kids are all back asleep," Allison says as she silently closes the bedroom door and walks back over toward her friend and husband. She pats Abigail's leg before sitting on the lap of Benjamin.

"Do you want to wake them up?" Benjamin asks as he puts his arm protectively around Allison.

"No, I am going to let them sleep, give them tonight. I will talk to them in the morning." Abigail says, choking back another sob.

The three huddle together on the couch, giving each other comfort.

"We will be right with you every step of the way, friend. Whatever you need, whenever you need it. We will be right there. You can count on us," Allison says, laying her head on Abigail's shoulder.

"I think I am going to go lay down with Brody. Snuggling with him helps me calm down. Maybe I will be able to get a few minutes of sleep."

"We will be right across the hall if you need anything! Don't worry about waking me up, just come get me if you need me." Allison says to Abigail as she gets up and walks toward the kid's bedroom.

"Thank you, goodnight."

"Goodnight, try to get some sleep," Benjamin offers as Allison grabs his hand and leads him toward their bedroom.

# CHAPTER 16

*A*bigail spent the entire night tossing and turning and begging her body to let her have just a few minutes of sleep. Holding onto Brody and listening to the soft breathing of her children gave her heart comfort amidst the turmoil she was going through. Getting up as quietly as she could so that she didn't wake up the kids, Abigail made her way out into the kitchen, Allison was already there making coffee.

"That smells delicious."

"I figured you didn't get any sleep last night and would need some brain fuel," Allison says offering a cup of liquid gold to Abigail with a small smile.

"You know me so well, thank you!"

"A lifelong friendship will do that, how are you feeling this morning?"

"Like my entire life has just imploded and all I want to do is lay down in bed and cry, but I have children, so I have to suck it up and pretend that I am fine, and we are all going to be okay. When in all actuality nothing about this is okay."

"Seems about right," Allison offers leaning up against the counter, taking a long swig of her own coffee concoction.

"When are you going to talk to the kids?" Benjamin asks joining the women in the kitchen.

"Later this morning I suppose. I just can't wrap my head around this. It can't be true, but then again, where could he be? Nothing is making sense anymore."

A few hours later, after they had all eaten breakfast and cleaned up the kitchen Abigail goes out onto the porch and calls for her kids to join her. Once they had all three sat down at the picnic table with their mother Abigail realized that this was it and the butterflies began fluttering all over her stomach and she was afraid she might throw up.

Benjamin and Allison stood in the doorway leading to the porch offering support. Abigail looks over to her friends, and Allison gives her a nod of assurance and mouths, "You got this."

*I need to get this over with, it's going to be hard, but the kids deserve the truth. They have been holding onto a sliver of hope that their daddy is going to be coming back, and I am going to take that away from them,"* she thinks to herself while taking a deep breath.

"I need all three of you guys to listen to me for a minute. Mommy needs to talk to you about something important," she sighs, trying to pull together her strength to make it through this conversation.

Once she has all of their attention, she begins the talk she never wanted to have with her kids. "Okay, I have some news that I need to discuss with you three."

"Is it about Daddy?" Madison asks, worried.

"Yes, sweetie, it *is* about Daddy, and before you start freaking out hear me out. I know what you are thinking and no, we do not have any reason to believe that anything bad happened to him," Abigail begins.

"Then where is he?" Madison asks loudly while throwing her hands into the air.

"Listen, honey, you know how the detective came by last

night, and we talked? Well, he was here to let us know that they have decided that they are going to stop the active search for Daddy."

"WHAT? Why? NO!" Madison wails.

"They think that daddy may have had a mental breakdown because of his medicine, and he just needed to get away for a little while," she explains softly.

"You mean, he really did just leave us?" Madison questions confused.

"Daddy doesn't want us anymore?" Brody whimpers.

"Oh, sweetie. I do not know what is going on in Daddy's mind right now. However, the one thing that I do know is that this is not any of your fault. The three of you are the absolute best part of everything in this world!" Abigail consoles.

"You're right mom; this is not our fault. It is all your fault!" Madison shouts angrily, jerking away from her mother.

"Excuse me, what did you just say to me?" Abigail replies, shocked.

Allison and Benjamin stand up straight in surprise, unsure if they should intervene, ultimately choosing to stand by and continue to watch this dramatic exchange unfold.

"You were always yelling at him and making him angry; he left us because he didn't want to be with you anymore! He left so he could live a life without arguing all the time," she yells as she storms into the house in tears.

Abigail sits stunned, silent, with tears brimming in her own eyes. She knew the kids would obviously be upset, but she never expected Madison to blame her.

"It's not your fault, Mommy," Kaitlyn offers as she and Brody lean into their mother, hugging her extra tight.

Benjamin, who had been silently standing in the doorway watching the, quietly follows Madison and gently knocks on her bedroom door.

"Go away," she yells angrily.

"Hey, it's just me. Do you mind if I talk to you for a minute?" he asks gently.

Madison opens the door and lets Benjamin inside; he walks over and sits on the edge of the bed opposite of Madison.

"Madison, you know that I think you and your siblings are so incredibly special, right? Allison and I both consider you all family. This is a horrible situation that you should not be going through, and I know that you are hurting right now, and for that, I am so sorry," he offers calmly.

"Why would my dad just leave me?" she cries.

"Your father has been my friend for a long time. This is so out of character for him. I honestly can't imagine what would cause him to do this to you guys. You are all extraordinary, but I do know that this is not your moms' fault, and I think deep down you know it too," he says gently.

"She was always so angry with him."

"We all make choices, and with those choices come consequences," he offers.

"Yeah," Madison sighs through her tears.

"No matter what the reason was that your dad left, that is on your dad. He made a choice to leave; therefore, it is no one's fault but his. You need your mom right now to help you get through this hurt and pain, but you know what, she needs you to help her get through the hurt too. She loves you more than you will ever know; don't turn on each other. Embrace and love each other!"

"It hurts so much," she whimpers.

"I know, and it is going to hurt for a long time, but each day that passes, it will get a little bit easier and a little bit easier. Allison and I will both be with you and your mom to get through it," he explains.

"Does my mom hate me?" she asked, worried.

"There is nothing you could ever do that would make your mom hate you, but you should probably go and apologize."

She nods her head in agreement and wipes away her tears before taking several deep breaths. Madison and Benjamin get up and walk out into the living room, where Abigail is sitting and cuddling with Kaitlyn and Brody on the couch. All of them were crying softly.

"I am sorry, Mom; I didn't mean what I said," Madison says, fidgeting with her fingers in front of her nervously. "My heart hurts."

"I know, sweetie. I know," her mother replies, letting her tears fall freely down her face. "Mine does too."

"Mommy, will you leave us too?" Kaitlyn asks terrified.

"NO! Baby no, I will never leave you, I promise!"

Madison sits down with her mom and pulls her into a bear hug before she starts crying into her shoulder. Abigail looks over to Benjamin and mouths the word thanks. Knowing that he was the one who went in there talked to the teenager and calmed her down. It is going to be a long hard road. They all sit there in silence, consoling each other. Finally, Benjamin looks to Allison, sitting on the chair, and motions for her to follow him outside, giving the family some privacy.

Once they get outside, Allison grabs hold of Benjamin frantically and pulls him into her chest, holding onto him tight. Her shoulders start to shake, and he realizes she is crying.

"What is it?" he asks, pulling back to look into her eyes, rubbing a thumb along her cheek and wiping away a tear.

"How are we going to help her get through this?"

"We will figure it out one day at a time," he says reassuringly as he plants a kiss on the tip of her nose.

"Why would Lucas do this to Abigail? How could he do this?" She continues as she places her head on his chest and cries. "Did you see the look in those kids' eyes?"

"Yeah, honestly, I just don't understand it. It is like he had a whole different life that we didn't see. I can't imagine how we were all so blind."

"She will never recover."

"Yes, she will. You will help her; we will help her. She isn't alone. None of them are."

"Kiss me. I need to feel something good," Allison says, leaning up on her toes and wrapping her arms around the neck of her husband.

"Gladly," he responds, meeting her lips with his own. Together they both pour all their love, worry, stress, and passion into that kiss. Allison pulls away to catch her breath and smacks Benjamin's butt before giving him another quick peck on the lips. "We should go and check on them, see if we can do anything. We are going to have to help them get home."

Benjamin nods in understanding and opens the back door to the cabin, following Allison inside.

# CHAPTER 17

*L*ucas wakes up with a splitting headache and stares up at the ceiling for a few minutes realizing that the dream he just awoke from was not the only nightmare he was dealing with. He was in fact living in a nightmare. Slowly rolling over as to not aggravate his headache any further he notices a water bottle and aspirin sitting on the side table next to the bed. He quickly popped the aspirin in his mouth and took a long swig of the cool water. Hoping for quick relief from the pain beating down in his skull.

Lucas, looking somber, stares at the tablet sitting on his lap while perched carefully on the edge of the bed. Benjamin is outside playing with his son. Abigail is in the kitchen taking care of the household duties alone. Is this so different from home? As he sits there in the dark room with only a vision of his family and his thoughts, he reflects on his life, thinking about all the things he did wrong, all the moments he missed, and all of the choices he has made up to this point in his life. "He shouldn't be playing ball with *my* son; I should be. But if I were there, would I be? Abigail shouldn't be alone. Did she feel alone in her own home, too?" Quietly he wonders as he lays back down, balancing the iPad on the bed in front of his face and against the side table so that he could watch his family while laying down. The last thing he sees is Abigail crying before he drifts back off to sleep.

A few hours later, he is awoken to the sound of a loud knock and realizes it is coming from the iPad, the knock is on the door at the cabin. He grabs a hold of the tablet and watches as Abigail opens the door for the detective. He continues to watch as he talks to Abigail. Watching her break down causes so much turmoil inside himself he leans over the side of the bed and throws up all over the floor.

"How can she believe this? Why doesn't she know how much I love her? I would never leave her."

He spends the next hour watching her cry and mourns the loss of their relationship, and an overwhelming sense of dread washes over him. Then, finally, he falls asleep watching the love of his life cry herself to sleep, and there is nothing he can do about it.

The following day, he wakes up with all of the same agonizing thoughts circling in his mind. Watching Abigail tell his children that he wasn't going to be returning home to them was the most painful thing he had ever seen. The heartbroken looks in his children's eyes were something he knew he would never be able to unsee.

As he watches everything unfold from the edge of his bed, Lucas comes to the realization that he is never going to be rescued or found. As he sits watching his family cry and mourn him leaving them, he is in total despair, knowing he wasted his chances with his family.

"Maybe John was right; I didn't deserve them. I didn't give them the best parts of me. I gave them whatever I had leftover. I should have been a better father; I should have been a better husband. They should have known deep in their souls that I loved them more than anything and that I would have never left them. Why didn't I spend quality time with them? Why didn't I put down my phone? They should have known! How could I let this happen? Why did I let this happen? I would give anything to fix my family. Dear God, I will do anything; please help me get out of here and let me correct all my wrongs. I will do right by my wife and my kids. I promise, I will change," he begs through his tears.

"Finally," John whispers from the shadows in the corner of the dark room.

John slowly saunters over to the bed and sits on the chair in front of Lucas.

"Good morning, Lucas how did you sleep last night?"

"I am not in the mood, what do you want?"

"Get up, we are going on a walk," John states matter-of-factly as he stands up, pushing the chair under the table and making his way over to the trick wall.

"Where are we going?"

"Let's just go without a bunch of annoying questions, it will make this go by so much faster."

Stopping and staring at John in panic, Lucas pulls up the courage to ask the burning question on his mind. "Are you going to kill me?"

"Lucas, what did I just say about stupid and annoying questions. Can we just go?"

*"I sure as hell am not going down without a fight,"* Lucas thinks to himself as he follows cautiously behind John out of the magic shop and toward the edge of town.

"Up we go," John says as he points to the ridge they are standing in front of.

"You want to go up the mountain?" Lucas asks confused.

"Seriously, you are an attorney? You can act so dumb, yes that is what I meant by up we go! Now up we go," he replies motioning for Lucas to get started walking up the trail leading up the ridge.

Once they reached the top, the view took Lucas's breath away. One side was a steep cliff, but it was nothing but trees and gorgeous mountains if you looked out past that edge. Lucas had never seen scenery so beautiful in his entire life.

"This is incredible," Lucas whispered.

"Yes, nature really can be quite lovely."

Suddenly wind began to blow, rustling the trees and flowing through their hair.

"Lucas, come back to me," was ever so faintly heard through the wind. Lucas began circling around frantically, searching all around him.

"Did you hear that?" He questioned still looking all around.

"Of course, I did."

"Where did it come from? Where are they? Lucas asks desperately.

"They aren't here," John replies taking two steps toward Lucas with a crazed look in his eye. Lucas took a few steps back to create distance between him and John, which caused him to be standing right on the edge of the cliff.

Panic crossed his face as he realized what John was going to do too late. In one swift motion John reached up with both hands and shoved Lucas over the edge.

"NOOOOOO...." Lucas screamed as he fell backwards arms straight out toward the ground below.

"I love you Lucas," was the last thing he faintly heard as he continued to fall. A small smile crept upon his face that the last thing he would hear before his death was a declaration of love from his wife.

# CHAPTER 18

eep

BEEP

BEEP

LUCAS BEGINS to wake up to the sound of an annoying beeping. He attempts to open his eyes, but he is no longer in darkness. Instead, he is surrounded by a bright light. His first thought is that he has died. He blinks rapidly to try and get his eyes to adjust to the light surrounding him. As his eyes begin to focus, the first thing he sees clearly is Abigail standing over him, worry evident on her face. She starts yelling and wiping away tears from her eyes. Grabbing ahold of his hand and squeezing tightly, she continues to scream. It takes a minute for him to understand what she is saying.

"Nurse, nurse, please get in here right away. Hurry! He is waking up!"

Struggling to comprehend what is happening, assuming he is in another awful nightmare, he lays his head back against his pillow and closes his eyes.

"No, baby, wakeup! Please, say something. The nurse is on her way now to check you out," Abigail says with relief, overjoyed that her husband had finally woken up.

"What? What nurse?" Lucas whispers with a raspy voice, pulling his hand up to his throat and rubbing it gently. His throat was parched and tender.

Abigail reached over to his bedside table and grabbed a small white Styrofoam cup. Then, turning the plastic straw toward him, she slowly brought it up to his lips.

"Here take a sip of water, it should help."

Looking all around the bright white room, which is a stark contrast to the black room that he has been being held in, Lucas finally realizes he is lying in a hospital bed with tubes and wires attached to different parts of his body. A middle-aged nurse comes running into the room with a huge smile plastered across her face.

"Good evening, Mr. Ferguson. Do you know where you are?" She asks as she begins checking his vitals.

He focuses all his attention on Abigail.

"Am I dreaming? How did you find me?" he asks, groggily and confused.

"Honey, you are at Cranston Creek Memorial Hospital. You had a heart attack and they had to rush you in for emergency surgery," she replies calmly, stroking his arm with her fingers softly.

"What? What do you mean? I don't understand, I didn't have a heart attack. What is going on? This must be another awful dream," he murmurs almost incoherently, becoming agitated.

"Hey, hey, calm down. You have to take it easy. You just had major surgery on your heart! Take a couple small breaths and relax. You are safe now."

Lucas begins rubbing his eyes and temples in confusion, trying to get clarity.

"I don't understand anything you are saying, I was being held captive in a room by that magic shop owner. How did you find me? The detective said they were not going to be looking for me anymore! I watched you guys; you were going to be moving on without me. You believed him when he said I left you," he rattles on in frustration.

Abigail looks up to the nurse, frantically unsure of what to do.

"Honey, listen to me carefully, you had a heart attack in the magic shop. You were rushed to the hospital for emergency surgery," she says slowly.

"Let me go get the doctor," the nurse says, panic crossing her face as she rushes out of the room.

"Babe, just rest; you are going to be okay now. After the doctor comes in and checks you out, I will call Allison to bring over the kids. They are going to be so happy you are finally awake. We were all so scared!"

"The kids! Where are the kids?" Lucas questions quickly.

"At the rental cabin with Allison and Benjamin, I called Allison on the way to the hospital, and they came right away. I don't know how I would have made it through these last couple of days without them honestly."

"So, I'm not dead?" Lucas asks as he grips Abigail's hand tightly, almost as if he let go, she would disappear.

Tapping on the top of his hand that is squeezing hers she gently loosens his grip. "No honey, you are not dead. It is a miracle, but thankfully you are still here with us!"

"Abigail, there are important things that I need to talk to you about. First, I need to tell you about a secret account I have been hiding for our future," Lucas begins his voice getting raspy again.

Okay, shhhh, now that you are awake, we can have those conversations. But not right now, later. Right now, you need to focus on rest and recovery!" she responds happily.

"I was not trying to hide things from you; I am sorry."

"Oh, my goodness, Lucas, trust me, the only thing I want to focus on right now is you getting better and all of us going home *together*. You have no idea how afraid I was that you wouldn't be coming home with us."

"I think I may have a better idea than you might think!" Lucas says in between coughs.

"The doctor says that if it weren't for the shop owner John catching you as you fell, it could have been so much worse. You were in surgery for almost 6 hours. It was touch and go, and the doctors told me that they thought they were going to lose you more than once! We were all just so incredibly scared! Oh, Lucas, I am so happy you are awake!" Abigail gushes, hugging her husband with relief. "I love you so much."

"But Abigail, what do you mean John saved me? He was the one that was holding me captive," he argues back, shaking his head in frustration.

"What? Captive? What are you talking about?" Abigail asks, cocking her head to the side.

The doctor walks into the room as Lucas is explaining his version of what happened to his wife. He listens intently to Lucas as he walks around the bed and begins checking the numbers on the machines that are currently hooked up to Lucas.

"Mr. Ferguson, you gave everyone quite the scare," he says, standing at the head of the bed looking down at the patient scrutinizing his pupils.

Lucas rubs his head and shakes it in frustration, looking back and forth from Abigail to the doctor.

"Doctor, I don't understand what is going on. Abigail's versions of what happened to me do not compute with my own. I was locked in a room, being held against my will. Watching Abigail and my kids on an iPad as they searched for me and cried that I had left them."

The doctor looks at him with nothing but care and crosses his arms across his chest calmly.

"Mr. Ferguson, what you are referring to is a very rare side effect of the anesthesia and medicine from your surgery. You were having a hallucinogenic dream. In your mind, what you thought you were living and seeing while you were under the influence of anesthesia was real, and so it may take you a few days to separate your dream from reality," the doctor explains calmly.

Lucas looks slowly at Abigail with tears in his eyes.

"So, none of it was real? You didn't think I abandoned you? I wasn't kidnapped? None of it?" he asks, relieved.

Abigail leans over to Lucas kisses his forehead gently.

"Oh, Abby, I am so sorry for the husband I have been. I promise I am going to do better; I am going to be better. For you and for the kids! Can you ever forgive me?" he begs.

Sweetly she rubs circles on his hands with her thumbs and says, "Of course I forgive you; I am just so happy you are awake and that you are going to be okay."

"I will give you a few minutes alone with your lovely wife, she has been right here by your side since you got here. Make sure you take it easy. No stress," the doctor says as he walks out the door.

"I am going to call Allison; the kids are going to be so happy. I am sure she will bring them right over!" Abigail says as she digs her phone out of her purse and calls her friend.

While Abigail is on the phone Lucas lays his head back against his pillow and glances out the window. It is evening so outside is dark, but he can see the stars twinkling against the black banket of the sky. There is one large star that is brighter than the rest that he focuses his attention on. He cannot explain why, but it brings him comfort. Peace, knowing that his nightmare is over and while it was awful, maybe it will make him a better man. One thing was for sure, he did not want his family to ever feel the way he saw them feeling in that nightmare. He was going to have make some real changes in his life.

"I am sorry, Abigail. I cannot tell you how ashamed I am of how I have been acting. You and the kids are everything to me. If I ever made you feel any less than that, I will spend the rest of my life making up for it," he whispered once she hung up her phone.

"Thankfully, you are alive and going to be okay to keep that promise!" Abigail smiles with relief.

Twenty minutes later, the door bursts open and the kids come rushing into the hospital room cheerfully.

"Daddy, Daddy, Daddy," they all chant happily.

"We sure are glad to see you are okay, Dad!" Madison says, relieved.

"Oh, here I thought I wasn't cool enough for you anymore," Lucas chided at his eldest daughter.

"You really aren't, but I still wanna keep you around," she laughed back total relief crossing her young features. Being able to see her dad back away and knowing he was going to be okay was a huge load lifted off her teenage shoulders.

Lucas smiles down at his family, thankful that he has this moment. Each of the kids take turns hugging their father in his hospital bed excitedly.

"I love you guys so much. You know that, right? You know that I would never leave you and that I love you more than anything."

"Yes, Daddy," they all reply in unison.

The doctor comes back in to check on Lucas. After going

over all his readings and watching his monitors, he smiles and nods his head.

"Everything is looking good. I am going to allow you to have just a few more minutes with your family, but you do have to rest and take it easy! We should have you back up on your feet so you can get back home in about a week or so. You can follow up with your family doctor once you are home," the doctor says as he walks out of the room, leaving the family alone, happily together.

Later that evening, after the children have all reluctantly left with Allison to go back to the cabin to get some sleep, Abigail rests on a chair with her hand firmly holding onto Lucas's. Sitting in a somewhat uncomfortable chair next to his bed, where she has been for the last several days, she begins to daydream about when they can go home. She looks over to her husband and stares at his face while he sleeps peacefully in his bed. The color has returned, and he was looking so much better. While she sits thanking the Lord for saving her husband, John enters the room quietly.

"Is it okay if I come in?" He questions, startling Abigail out of her silent prayer.

"Hi, John! It is so good to see you again!" She exclaims as he enters the room with a smile. "Thank you again for helping to save Lucas," she continues as she pulls her hand from Lucas's and stands to greet the visitor. "I don't know that he would be here with us today if it weren't for your quick actions!"

Lucas, hearing voices in his room talking slowly opens his sleepy eyes, once he recognizes John his eyes go wide, and he stares at John in sheer terror.

"It was really my pleasure, Mrs. Ferguson. I am so happy that I was there and able to help. Please don't think anything of it. I was wondering if you would mind if I had a word with Mr. Ferguson for a minute? Alone?"

"No, Abigail, you can stay in here with me," Lucas attempts to shout, but his voice is barely above a whisper.

"Don't be silly, your wife I'm sure could use a minute to stretch her legs after being cramped in this room for the last few days, besides it will be quick," John argues entering further into the room.

"It is totally fine, Lucas honey, I will be right back. I would actually like to go down the hall and get a snack; I'm starving, I haven't really eaten the entire time we have been here," she replies while standing up and kissing Lucas on the top of his head before walking toward to door. "No more funny business mister," she scolds her husband teasingly as she walks away.

"Lucas," John begins as Lucas stares back in fear. "I am glad to see you are feeling better and are awake. You gave everyone quite the scare."

"What are you doing here?" Lucas asks while reaching for the call light in case things go awry.

"Oh Lucas, you are not going to need that. So untrusting."

"I will keep it close, just in case if you don't mind. Now answer my question, what are you doing in here?"

"Suit yourself," John laughed and shrugged nonchalantly. "I just wanted to stop by to check on you and let you know that while it did take you a bit longer than I expected it to, I am glad that you finally understood what I was trying to teach you."

Lucas started back at John in bewilderment. "Wait. "*You*, you did this to me? You gave me a heart attack? Almost killed me?" Lucas demands angrily.

"Don't be ridiculous; you were going to have the heart attack either way. I just capitalized on the opportunity to show you the error of your ways. Giving you the chance to change your future before what you witnessed became a reality," John explains, exasperated.

"What if I never realized I needed to change?" Lucas asks.

"Well, then, unfortunately, you would have left your family

forever, and we would not be here having this conversation. Thankfully though, you did, and here we are."

"What do you mean? I would have died?"

"Sadly, yes, you would have died on that operating table. Ask the doctors, it was very touch and go there for a while as it was. When you took off running, and then later instead of listening to me you just wanted to fight. Sigh. Allowing you to go back to your family an unchanged man would not have been fair to anyone. Keeping on the same path was not an option," John explains with a shrug.

"Why would you get to decide that? You don't even know me!"

"Who said I was the one deciding? I told you from the beginning, that I wasn't the one keeping you, I was just the one watching over you."

"*Who* are you?" Lucas asks quietly.

John just looks at him and shrugs as Abigail walks back in. "I am just a magic store owner, doing my best to better the lives of the patrons that enter my shop."

Abigail smiles at John cheerfully as she enters the room, arms filled with vending machine snacks. She gets drops all of the junk food onto the side table and wiggles back into her chair trying to get comfortable again. "Sorry, John, I couldn't stay away too long. I had to check in on the patient."

"Totally understandable Mrs. Ferguson. I am relieved that he is going to be okay! Go home and enjoy your family, enjoy each other, your children, and every day you have. You never know when it will be your last. Don't let the people you care about wonder if you loved them after you are gone. Spend your time here on this earth making sure they know, while you are still here. Make your story one for the ages!" John says as he walks back out of the hospital room.

# CHAPTER 19

$\mathcal{A}$t the end of the following week, the Ferguson family pull into their driveway back at home. The children jump out of the car and run into the house while Abigail helps Lucas towards the front door.

"Mom, can I invite Tony over?" Madison yells from the front steps.

"Seriously? Madison we just got home like 30 seconds ago."

"But Mom, I haven't seen him in almost two weeks!" Madison whines back with her big puppy dog eyes.

"Okay honey, fine. But you guys have to keep it down Daddy still needs his rest."

"Thank you, thank you!" she squeals as she continues to run off into the house.

"It feels so good to be back home," Lucas says warmly, wrapping his arm tightly around his wife.

"It feels good to have you back home, safe and sound!" Abigail replies with relief in her voice.

"What do you say we plan a real family vacation?" Lucas asks as they walk into their house.

"I would say that sounds wonderful, but no heart attacks this time!" She chuckles while pretending to slug him in the arm.

"I would be happy to make that deal!"

Beep beep. They hear as Allison and Benjamin pull into their own driveway next door. Abigail had told them that they could go ahead and go back home a few days earlier, but they were insistent that they were going to wait and caravan with them home, just to make sure everything was okay.

Abigail lifted her arm and waived at the couple as they grabbed their bags and headed into their own house.

"Call me if you need anything hon," Allison shouts as she closes her front door behind them.

Lucas spent the next few days resting and reflecting on his life and the changes that he needed to make to better his life and the lives of his family. Finally, after much thought and planning, he was ready to discuss his decisions with Abigail. That evening, while Lucas is resting on their bed, finding himself alone with his thoughts once again, he begins to talk to himself quietly unconsciously. Looking around his bedroom at the pictures of his family hanging on the walls and scattered on furniture throughout the room, he has an overwhelming sense of relief.

"I am going to change my life. I promise, I am going to be a better family man. I was given a second chance, and I am not going to take it for granted," he promises to no one in particular. "I will prove to everyone that I am deserving of this family. Of this gift."

Abigail walks out of the bathroom brushing through her wet hair and in her pajamas. She smiles lovingly at Lucas while finishing getting ready for bed.

"You okay, babe?" She asks casually as she rubs lotion across her neck and face.

"Honestly, honey, I have never been better! Even though I just had a heart attack, I feel like I have this new lease on life. I can see everything so much more clearly. My priorities have all changed. I am looking forward to the future," he replies happily.

Abigail sits next to him on the bed, leans over, and kisses him gently.

"That is so great to hear, and I will be right here with you every step of the way."

"I love you, Abigail."

"I love you too," she replies while laying down and snuggling up close to her husband a smile of contentment on her face.

A familiar buzzing can be heard from across the room near the dresser. Abigail shifts her gaze in that direction and can see the light illuminating from her husband's phone. "Do you want me to get that?" She asks politely.

Lucas who is laying back comfortably cuddling with his wife shakes his head no, plants a kiss on the top of her head and closes his eyes restfully.

"They can leave a message if they need me, I will check it in the morning. Kevin is still handing things for me at the office. Let's just relax and enjoy our evening."

"Wow, he really is a new Lucas. The old Lucas would have dashed to his phone to answer it immediately," she thinks to herself curiously.

"Kaitlyn has a dance recital this week doesn't' she?" He asks sleepily.

"Yeah, it's on Thursday, why are you going to go?" Abigail asks cautiously. Lucas has never once been to any of the kid's extracurriculars. He justified his absence by reminding her that his work was what paid for them in the first place, so in a way, he was there."

"Mmhmm," he replied drifting off to sleep. "I would really like to go; I'm looking forward to it."

Abigail closed pulled the blanket up to her chin, closing her eyes in complete contentment. Afraid to become too hopeful that this was the breakthrough she had been praying for, but cautiously optimistic, nonetheless.

The next couple of weeks go by slowly, with Lucas and the family mostly hanging out around the house, helping him recover. Lucas did in fact attend Kaitlyn's recital, going so far as to order her flowers to be delivered to the house while they were gone. The happiness on her face was more than any dollar amount could buy the father. One night, before going to bed, Lucas calls Abigail into his. home office, where he is sitting behind his desk.

"I need to go see Michael at the office tomorrow," Lucas says as he closes the file he has open in front of him.

"Are you sure that is a good idea? You are supposed to stay away from stress, it hasn't been that long since your surgery. I thought you gave his case to one of the other attorneys in your office."

"I did, and I know that Kevin is more than capable of handling the case, I am not going to take it back from him, but after everything I went through, I would really like to speak with Michael again."

"Okay, if you are sure you are up for it. Just remember to take it easy. Don't get too excited or upset; your heart is still recovering."

"I promise, I will be very aware and cautious my love. Now, why don't you come with me to bed so we can have some alone time together," he requests while rising from his chair and grabbing ahold of her hand, leading her down the hall.

A broad smile graces Abigail's face as she follows him happily. While she would never wish a heart attack or any other type of near-death experience on her husband, she has taken notice of the tremendous changes in him since he has been home. He has been everything she had been hoping he would be and knew he could be.

Early the following morning, Lucas makes his way down the

familiar hall of the Ferguson Law Office, to meet with Michael and his parents. Stopping along the way to offer a good morning to each of the members of his staff before entering the gorgeous conference room overlooking the downtown area. This has always been one of his favorite rooms in his building as he enjoyed the floor-to-ceiling windows offering a picturesque view. Walking into the room, he smiled generously at Michael and his parents, who were already waiting and seated when he arrived.

"Geez, dude, what happened to you?" Michael says, stunned at the appearance of Lucas. He has lost quite a bit of weight since his heart attack and had obviously not been going to the gym, so his body had been taking on a few changes recently.

"Michael, manners!" His mother scolds embarrassed.

"No, I mean he looks like he is sick! That is not what he looked like when he came to visit me at the jail!"

"Shut up son, you are not helping yourself." His father chimes in.

"I apologize, I didn't mean anything by it. I was just surprised is all. I hope you aren't actually sick and that's why you put that Kevin guy on my case instead."

"Michael, I told you Mr. Ferguson called us and let us know he was taking some personal time, but his associate was equally as good and would be helping you out. I am so sorry, Mr. Ferguson I don't know what has gotten into his mouth today," the mother responds clearly embarrassed by her sons' outbursts.

"Well, you could say I have been through an ordeal. But thankfully I am going to be okay! I have been given a second chance at life, and I am focusing on making it the best version of life for my family and me. Now, I am here to talk to you about making sure you are okay. That you have something to look forward to in the future."

Michael looks down at his hands, refusing to reply.

"I know you have been giving my associate the cold shoulder and not answering any of his questions. But, Michael, you have to know that we want to help you."

"I already told you I don't deserve your help."

"Michael, this isn't going to go away. There are going to be dire consequences for what happened. One of them is the torture that you are putting yourself through. Please let us help you with the court proceedings."

Michael looks up at Lucas with tears brimming in his eyes.

"Look around, your parents are so worried about you, they are here beside you wanting to walk this road with you. They are trying to help you through this. You do not have to go through this alone. Listen to me when I tell you, I have made mistakes in my life, and I was given a second chance to fix them. You are so young; your life is not over. There can be a life after this."

"I loved her."

"I have no doubt you did. It was a horrible accident."

"An accident that I caused, it was one hundred percent my fault," he whispered as tears began filling his soft green eyes.

"I am not going to lie to you and tell you that what you did was not stupid, horrible and tragic. You are going to get some jail time for this. I am glad you are in personal counseling to go along with the alcohol classes you are taking. Use this opportunity to turn your life around, honor the memory of her, teach other young people the dangers of texting and driving and drinking and driving. We all hear it, but no one ever thinks it is going to happen to them. You are a testament that it can."

"Why do you even care about what happens to me?"

"You are so young; I want to see you turn your life around and do something great. Don't wait until it is too late to realize you could have been out there making a difference. Serve your time, get your life together and then go out there and change the world."

"Thank you, Mr. Ferguson," Michaels's father says as he stands and offers his hand.

"It is my pleasure; my associate will take good care of your son. If you guys need anything let me know."

"I want to make my parents proud," Michael says turning around and talking to Lucas.

"I have no doubt that once you get this behind you, they are going to be so proud of you and what you accomplish with the rest of your life," Lucas offers patting him on the back reassuringly as they continue to walk out of the office.

Walking outside, Lucas took a deep breath of the warm air and smiled at the woman sitting behind the steering wheel inside his car. Abigail was quietly reading and patiently waiting for him to finish his meeting.

"How did it go?" she asks curiously as Lucas slid into the passenger seat.

"Better than expected. I really think he is going to be okay."

Lovingly she leans over and kisses Lucas passionately. "You are amazing; you know that? I am so incredibly proud of you."

"That means more to me than any case or award I could ever win," Lucas replies happily.

"Benjamin and Allison have invited us over for dinner tonight if you are up for it."

"Sounds good. I am feeling great today actually, I really owe them for jumping in and helping you while I was out of it. They proved to be the best of friends."

"That they did."

That night after Abigail had fed the kids and gotten them settled, she and Lucas set off on a walk next door to enjoy an evening of food and fellowship with their friends. As they walk by the front window toward the front door, they are surprised to see Allison and Benjamin locked in a passionate embrace in the middle of the living room.

Abigail and Lucas both start laughing at the scene in front of them. "If we leave them to it a few more minutes this may become X rated," Abigail snorts through her laughter.

Lucas taps the window instead of ringing the doorbell, causing Allison to jump and shriek in surprise. Benjamin doubles over in laughter and opens the front door.

"Uh, should we come back later?" Lucas asks, laughing.

"No, we were just celebrating!" Allison says, slightly embarrassed but happy at the same time.

"Spill it!" Abigail demands as they walk into the front door and head to the living room together.

"Oh, it's nothing," she coyly responds turning her back to the group and walking further into the living room.

"ALLISON MARIE, you turn around and look me in the eye and tell me what has you so excited and celebrating right this instant," Abigail jokingly yells as she bounces up and down on her tippy toes in anticipation.

"No use in pretending baby, you know darn well you are going to crack with her anyway," Benjamin laughs putting his arm around Lucas carefully and leaning toward his ear. "Wait until you hear this!"

Lucas looks at him and smiles eagerly awaiting the news. "Okay now I am curious too, what is going on?"

"Well, it is very early, and I don't want anyone else to know, but I am pregnant!" Allison yells while jumping up and down, grabbing a hold of Abigail and hugging her tightly.

Tears begin streaming down Abigail's face. She knows how much this means to her friend. Throughout all the failed treatments and negative tests Abigail has been right there holding her hand and letting her cry on her shoulder. Allison and Benjamin had been trying to have a baby for years and had all but given up hope that they would ever become parents. A year earlier they had decided to stop treatments settling for the fact that it was probably not in the cards for them, so the fact that they were able to finally get pregnant on their own was another miracle that Abigail was going to be praising God for.

"Oh my gosh, honey, I am so happy for you guys!"

"Congratulation's man!" Lucas says while slapping Benjamin on the back. "You are going to make an incredible father!"

"Thanks, Lucas, that really means a lot!"

"I mean it man; you are a good dude. I know you guys have been down a long road to get here, but I am truly so happy for you both."

"Okay, I get to plan your shower, ohhhhh I am going to be an auntie!" Abigail squealed in delight.

"Slow down silly, it's too early to be planning anything, but YEAH!" Allison laughed while hugging her best friend again happily.

The rest of the evening is spent laughing, eating, and enjoying each other's company, all while not one person picked up or used a single electronic device the entire night.

"Thanks for having us over tonight you guys, it was a great time. Thanks for sharing your big news with us too!" Abigail says cheerfully as they stand on the front steps getting ready to head back home.

"Goodnight!" Lucas waves as he wraps his arm around Abigail and leads her across the grass to their house next door.

After they are back home and tucked into their bed, Lucas grabs ahold of Abigail and pulls her into his chest carefully. She rests her head on him listening to the sound of his heart beating. Lately it has been her favorite thing to do when they are lying in bed quietly alone.

"Baby, I needed to run an idea I have been working on lately by you," he whispers, running his hand through her hair.

"Sure, what is it?"

"How would you feel about me partially retiring. I would still help the associates and take a case now and then. But the law practice makes more than enough money for us to live on comfortably without me having to take on such an active role. That would give us so much time to just spend together as a family. Just making memories together."

Abigail slowly looks up to her spouse and kisses him long and hard.

"Or we could talk about the first thing that pops up." Lucas laughs as she pulls away from the kiss. "So, does that mean you are okay with it?

"It sounds wonderful. I love you so much, Lucas."

"I love you too, sweetheart," he says, kissing her on the top of the head. "There is one more thing I need to talk to you about. I started to tell you about it at the hospital and have just not gotten around to finishing that conversation. I don't want you to be upset or think I have been keeping something from you. Not maliciously, but, well the thing is I have been storing away money. I was saving it for when I retired. I wanted to surprise you and travel the world together, just the two of us after the kids were grown," he says as he looks down at her to gauge her reaction.

"Wow, that's wonderful. How much is in it?" she asks casually, in her mind she is expecting fifty thousand or so maybe less but certainly not more. She was not entirely sure how long he had been saving.

Lucas cleared his throat and whispered, "Three-quarters of a million dollars."

Abigail looks up at him with her mouth hanging open. "I'm sorry, I think I misunderstood you. How much?"

Lucas chuckles at her while pulling her back down to his chest. "See, I told you we will be just fine."

# CHAPTER 20

## FLASHING THROUGH MOMENTS OF THEIR LIFE

*\* The family is laughing and smiling together as they have a backyard BBQ. Playing and enjoying each other's company, and just being present and attentive with one another.*

*ENJOYING A BEACH VACATION, Lucas plays ball with Brody while Abigail and the girls build sandcastles. Abigail looks over lovingly at Lucas and smiles. This new attentive and present Lucas is absolutely what she had always hoped and prayed for. Finally, her husband was back, and their life was so much happier for it.*

*SEVERAL MONTHS LATER, the family gathers in the kitchen to celebrate Lucas's birthday. Everyone is smiling, happy, and laughing while Lucas blows out the candles on the cake.*

Smiling and putting her arms around her husband before

kissing him gently, Abigail looks at her family. "This birthday is extra special because just a few short months ago, I wasn't sure if we would even have this day."

"I definitely learned not to take a single day for granted this year, and I want to live my life with purpose and be present every single day," he responds lovingly, stroking her hair off her face.

*A FEW YEARS LATER, the Ferguson family is again celebrating a birthday in their kitchen, only this time it is for Kaitlyn, who is turning 16 years old. As she leans over and blows out the candles on the cake, Lucas begins to dangle keys in front of her, and she screams in excitement.*

"Are you serious?" she shrieks, running to her father and giving him a bear hug and grabbing the keys from his hand.

"Let's go see what you got!" Abigail says with a huge smile, and she starts walking out the front door

Kaitlyn stands in the driveway with her mouth hanging wide open in surprise. Everyone stands and stares at the brand-new Tesla sitting in the driveway waiting for its new owner.

"This is my dream car!" she yells, running toward the car with sheer joy.

Abigail and Lucas stand hand-in-hand and watch the smile on their daughter's face as she shows her car to her brother and sister happily.

*ONE AFTERNOON, Lucas and Abigail walk into the high school auditorium. They are going to have a special guest speaker for all the kids at the school, and the couple wanted to be in attendance. So, after finding their seats, they watch as Michael Huntsman walks onto the stage and up to the microphone.*

"Thank you all for coming! My name is Michael, and I am

here to talk to you about choices and how they can affect the rest of your lives," he begins. "I know you are probably thinking that this is going to be another lecture about college, but trust me, it's not. However, it may be one of the most important lessons you ever listen to, and I hope you all walk away from this with a newfound ideal of fun and responsibility. Because while you may not think anything bad will ever happen to you, it can, and if you make bad choices like I did, it probably will."

Lucas looks to Abigail with a proud smile. "I knew he was going to do something good with his life."

*A FEW SHORT MONTHS LATER, it is college graduation day for Madison. They stand in the auditorium proudly as they watch Madison walk across the stage and accept her diploma. The happy parents are able to take a few pictures with Madison in her cap and gown before she runs off with her friends.*

"I can't believe she's graduated college already; she is all grown up!" Abigail says with a tinge of sadness in her voice as they watch her laugh and goof off with her schoolmates in celebration.

Madison looks over and offers a smile and a wave before running in the opposite direction with her friends.

*ONE EVENING, Abigail and Lucas are watching a teenage Brody playing basketball in a high school gym. Abigail and Lucas jump up and begin loudly cheering as Brody makes a shot, and it banks in, causing his team to win the game at the buzzer.*

*IT'S PROM NIGHT, and Kaitlyn slowly comes walking down the hallway, all dressed up in her beautiful prom dress. Abigail is taking pictures of her while Lucas looks on, smiling proudly at his daughter.*

. . .

*LUCAS AND ABIGAIL* stand over Brody, sitting at the kitchen table, staring at an envelope. He is afraid to see what is inside. Abigail puts her hands gently on his shoulders, and he begins to open it slowly and read the letter. He jumps for joy while letting out a squeal of pure relief. Lucas and Abigail embrace him, and all three jump around happily. The letter floats onto the table; it is a college acceptance letter to Indiana University Bloomington, his number one choice school.

*A FEW YEARS LATER*, a handsome young man stands at an altar with a minister. Abigail smiles warmly at him before turning with the rest of the crowd to see Lucas and Madison walking down the aisle. Lucas kisses Madison on the cheek, and she walks up to her groom ready to be married.

*THE FOLLOWING YEAR*, Brody is standing at the altar with Lucas standing right next to him as his best man. They shake hands and turn to see a beautiful bride begin her walk down the aisle.

*LATER THAT SAME YEAR*, Kaitlyn is in a gorgeous wedding gown, standing outside the church interior doors with her father. She turns to him and gives him a bear hug before the door opens, and she begins her walk with Lucas down the aisle toward her groom.

*TWO YEARS LATER*, Madison is lying in a hospital bed sweating profusely. Abigail is on one side of her, and her husband is standing on the other. A doctor walks in, putting on gloves as he smiles at Madison.

"OK, it's time to start pushing," he says.

"You got this, Madison. Just breathe," Abigail tells her daughter while squeezing her hand and willing her strength.

A few short hours later, Abigail and Lucas sit in the hospital room with their daughter and son-in-law, cuddling with their first grandchild.

*MANY YEARS LATER, the entire Ferguson family is in the backyard enjoying a delicious BBQ. All three of the children, spouses, and many, many grandchildren. The children are running throughout the yard, playing while the adults sit around and watch, smiling and laughing.*

"This is what it is all about," Lucas whispers to Abigail while he looks at his family happily. "I can't believe I almost missed it."

"This is what it is all about, and I am glad you are still here with us to be a part of each. Moment." Abigail agrees, smiling and leaning into him.

# CHAPTER 21

*L*ucas and Abigail, now in their 80's, are sitting on their front porch swing looking out over their front yard, where a few of their grandkids are riding bikes in front of their home.

"Faith honey don't ride to far away on your bike, Grandma can't see you," Abigail yells to her ten-year-old granddaughter as she watches her ride to the edge of the cul-de-sac.

"Don't worry grandma, I know the rules," Faith hollers back as she does a loop with her bike and heads back towards her grandparents' house.

"Dad, the grill is all fired up, so I am going to start cooking the burgers now, Madison just texted that she finally got the kids loaded in the car, so she and Tony are on their way," Brody said as he peeked his head out of the front door holding onto a plate of raw hamburger meat and a spatula.

"Thanks son, you need any help?"

"No dad, relax with mom, I got this," Brody said walking back into the house and letting the door smack shut behind him.

Lucas and Abigail swing in silence and watch the kids

playing and laughing. A content sigh escapes Abigail's lips as she lays her head on the shoulder of her beloved.

"Abby, we sure have had a good life together, haven't we?" he asked, smiling.

"Blessed beyond measure, my love. It has been a really great life, honey. We have two amazing kids, their spouses, and all our grandkids; we have traveled all over the world and seen things most people only dream about. What we created has been a once-in-a-lifetime love," she replies, reaching for his hand and squeezing gently.

"I am so glad I met you that night at the club so long ago. You really have been the love of my life. Thank you for never giving up on us, sweetheart."

"Oh, Lucas, I love you just as much now as I ever have. Meeting you that night was the beginning of my life."

Lucas leans over and kisses her forehead gently, and they rock, and rock, and rock. "We made our love story one for the ages."


THE END